D0589129

NELLIE
and the Dragon
— Whatever Next? —

"Hello, Nellie, it's me," Gertrude called across the shop. She was balancing with one leg on top of a clothes model wearing a track suit. The model's head was wobbling horribly. Nellie could see that at any moment it was going to break. She shut her eyes. Then suddenly there was a terrific crash as the model collapsed. Gertrude ended up in a tangle of plastic legs and arms and track suit.

"Goodness," said the shop assistant serving Nellie and Dad. "It's collapsed. I've never known anything like that happen before."

That's because it's never had a dragon standing on its head before, thought Nellie.

Also by Elizabeth Lindsay in Hippo Books:

Nellie and the Dragon
Heggerty Haggerty and the Amazing Loaf of Bread
Heggerty Haggerty and the Day at the Fair
Heggerty Haggerty and the Flying Saucer
Heggerty Haggerty and the Great Running Race
Heggerty Haggerty and the Hallowe'en Ghost
Heggerty Haggerty and the Magic Medicine
Heggerty Haggerty and the Treasure Hunt

NELLIE
and the Dragon
— Whatever Next? —

Elizabeth Lindsay

Illustrated by
Jim Hodgson

Hippo Books
Scholastic Publications Limited
London

Scholastic Publications Ltd.,
10 Earlham Street, London WC2H 9RX, UK

Scholastic Inc.,
730 Broadway, New York, NY 10003, USA

Scholastic Tab Publications Ltd.,
123 Newkirk Road, Richmond Hill,
Ontario L4C 3G5, Canada

Ashton Scholastic Pty. Ltd.,
P O Box 579, Gosford, New South Wales,
Australia

Ashton Scholastic Ltd.,
165 Marua Road, Panmure, Auckland 6,
New Zealand

First published by Scholastic Publications Limited, 1989

Text copyright © Elizabeth Lindsay, 1989
Illustrations copyright © Jim Hodgson, 1989

10 9 8 7 6 5 4 3 2 1

ISBN 0 590 76026 2

Made and printed by Cox and Wyman Ltd.,
Reading, Berks.

Typeset in Times by COLLAGE (Design in Print)
Longfield Hill, Kent.

Contents

1 Nellie Goes Shopping   1
2 Nellie and the Flying
   Umbrella   14
3 Nellie and the Birthday
   Surprise   26
4 Nellie Goes Swimming   39
5 Nellie and the Tree Den   52
6 Nellie and the Mystery Box   64
7 Nellie and the Uncatchable
   Hat   77
8 Nellie Buys a Kite   89
9 Nellie and the Runaway
   Skateboard   104
10 Nellie Goes to the Seaside   116

For Claire and Tom

1 Nellie Goes Shopping

It was Saturday. Dad was taking Nellie shopping. Granny May was taking Meg the dog for a walk in the park. There was a jumble of people and dog in the hall, and it got more confusing on the pavement as Meg jumped into the car with Nellie.

"No, Meg," said Nellie. "You're going to the park with Granny May." Meg jumped out again. Granny May had to go back indoors. She'd forgotten Meg's ball. Meg barked, "Woof, woof," which meant "Hurry up."

"No barking, Meg," said Nellie. But Meg wouldn't listen. Going to the park was fun and

1

she wanted to get there.

"Woof, woof, woof, woof, woof," she barked. Nellie put her hands over her ears.

"For goodness sake, do something about that dog," said Dad.

"I can't," said Nellie. "I've tried."

"It's all right. I've found it," said Granny May. She held up the red ball. "Meg had hidden it in her basket." Meg jumped up and Granny May dropped the ball into her mouth for her to carry.

"Thank goodness for that," said Dad, as the barking stopped. "Whatever will the neighbours think?"

"They'll think it's a mad house," said Granny May, laughing. "Come on, Meg."

Nellie watched Meg trot along the pavement beside Granny May, her tail wagging happily.

"I wish I could go to the park too," Nellie said.

"Maybe later," said Dad. "It's shopping first."

Floyd, Nellie's friend from next door, waved to them from his front-room window. Nellie pulled a funny face at him. Floyd pulled one back, and they both laughed.

"Can't play," shouted Nellie. "Going shopping!" Floyd nodded.

"So that's what they're up to," said a curious

voice from the roof of Nellie's house. "I wondered what all the commotion was about. Shopping sounds like fun." The voice belonged to Gertrude the dragon. Gertrude lived in the old shed at the bottom of Nellie's garden.

As Dad started the engine, Gertrude flew from the roof and landed neatly on top of the car. Nellie heard the thud as they were driving off. She looked out of the back window and saw the end of Gertrude's tail swaying behind them. Dad looked in his mirror. He didn't see Gertrude's tail, only the car that was following them.

Gertrude always said, "It's only believers who see us and most people don't." Nellie believed in dragons and so did Meg and Sam, Granny May's black-and-white cat. No one else seemed to. Not Dad, or Granny May, or even Floyd.

Dad drove them to the big car park in the shopping precinct. At the barrier he took his ticket from the machine and the barrier lifted. Nellie heard a squeal of delight from the roof. Dad drove the car into the car park, and the barrier came down behind them. Nellie looked back and was surprised to see Gertrude sitting on the barrier. When the next car reached the barrier the driver took the ticket but the barrier didn't lift.

"Gertrude's weighing it down," said Nellie.

"She wants a ride but she's too heavy." The car driver got out and went to fetch the car park attendant. Gertrude got fed up with waiting and jumped down. The barrier went up.

"What's wrong with it?" the attendant asked. "It's working all right." The driver looked confused and got back in the car.

"It wasn't," he said.

Dad and Nellie were already in the lift when a voice said, "Wait for me!"

"Too late!" said Nellie. The lift doors were closing. A golden clawed foot suddenly appeared between the doors and they opened again. Gertrude squashed herself inside. Dad was surprised. There was no one there, yet suddenly the lift seemed very full.

"Why didn't you tell me you were going shopping, Nellie? You know a dragon is partial to a little outing." Nellie didn't say anything in case Dad thought she was talking to herself. He often did when she was talking to Gertrude.

"What are you going to buy? Come on, speak up. I want to know what's what and where we're off to. Are you going to the toy shop? I did enjoy playing with that bouncy ball last time we went." Nellie went hot and cold as she remembered Gertrude and the bouncy ball.

"No," she said. "We're not buying toys, we're getting me some new trainers and an anorak."

"That's right," said Dad. "You can go to the toy department if there's time."

"Goody," said Gertrude.

"No, it's all right, Dad, really," said Nellie.

When they got out of the lift, Dad led the way to the big department store where Nellie was going to try on trainers and anoraks. Nellie, looking over her shoulder, saw Gertrude following along behind.

Inside the store they walked across the ground floor, passing the food store and the ladies' hat department. The childrens' department was upstairs. Nellie stopped at the sweet counter and was about to ask Dad if she could buy some toffees when she saw Gertrude wearing a long brown wig and trying on a bright

5

green, lacy hat.

"Gertrude!" Nellie gasped. There were startled cries from the customers as Gertrude stood before the mirror in first one pose and then another. They couldn't see the dragon but they could see a floating wig and hat swaying before them.

"Gertrude, take them off, you're causing a sensation!" cried Nellie. But Gertrude couldn't hear above the noisy panic she was surrounded by.

The shop manager advanced with a broom and bravely knocked the hat and wig from Gertrude's head. If only he'd known a dragon was underneath them. Gertrude was furious. Dressing up was fun. She took a deep breath and burnt the broom to a cinder, causing the startled shop manager to drop it. He jumped on the glowing embers which were scorching the carpet.

"Fetch a fire extinguisher!" he shouted. Nellie groaned. Dad stared amazed. He'd never seen anything like it in his life.

"Did you see that? The broom burst into flames," said Dad.

"It was the dragon," said Nellie.

"Extraordinary," said Dad. "If I hadn't seen it I wouldn't have believed it."

"No need to panic, ladies and gentlemen," said the shop manager. "Everything is under control."

Under control, thought Nellie, smiling. Some hopes with Gertrude around!

Gertrude gave up trying on hats. "I'm coming with you, Nellie," she said.

"Why can't you behave yourself?" said Nellie. "It's no fun having you around when you cause so much trouble."

Dad led the way to the escalator, followed by Nellie, who was followed by Gertrude.

"I promise to be good," said Gertrude.

"The trouble with you is that you don't know what good is," said Nellie.

Gertrude did behave on the way up the escalator. But she enjoyed the ride so much she wanted another go. She flew down again over the heads of the people coming up, causing such a draught with her wings that a lady's hat blew off. When she reached the ground floor Gertrude jumped on once again. So did a man in a hurry believing there to be a space. He bumped into Gertrude who gave him a shove with her bottom. The man landed in a heap at the foot of the escalator, wondering why he'd fallen off. Gertrude had three goes on the escalator before hopping off for the last time.

"That was fun," she said. "I wonder where Nellie is?"

Nellie was trying on anoraks. She'd tried on a green one and had on a red one. There was a yellow one and a blue-and-purple one left to try.

"Hello, Nellie, it's me," Gertrude called across the shop. She was balancing with one leg on top of a clothes model wearing a track suit. The model's head was wobbling horribly. Nellie could see that at any moment it was going to break. She shut her eyes. Suddenly there was a terrific crash as the model collapsed. Gertrude ended up in a tangle of plastic legs and arms and track suit.

"Goodness," said the shop assistant serving Nellie and Dad. "It's collapsed. I've never known anything like that happen before."

That's because it's never had a dragon standing on its head before, thought Nellie, but she didn't say anything. She watched as Gertrude got up sheepishly from amongst the ruin she had caused.

"Sorry, Nellie," she said. Nellie ignored her.

"I was only showing you how good a dragon is at balancing," she said. "Look at this." Gertrude leaned back onto her tail and wriggled her arms and legs in the air. She looked so funny that Nellie couldn't help laughing.

"Nice to see a smile on your face, Nellie," said Gertrude.

The manager was called by the assistant to look at the broken model. He looked grim. He couldn't understand why it had broken.

"We seem to have a vandal in the shop. One who likes playing tricks," he said. "Keep your eyes peeled. We don't want them to get away."

"Dad, can I have the red anorak?" said Nellie.

"Don't you want to try the others on?" Dad asked.

"No, the red one'll be fine."

When the shop assistant came back, Nellie tried on some blue trainers. They fitted.

"Can I have these, Dad?"

"Don't you want to try any others?" Dad asked. Nellie didn't. She wanted to get out of the shop as fast as possible. Although no one seemed to be able to see Gertrude, she didn't like the thought of her being a vandal. A vandal could be arrested and sent to prison. Why, oh why did Gertrude have to be so naughty?

Dad paid the shop assistant for the anorak and trainers.

"Can we go home now, Dad?" said Nellie.

"Don't you want to go to the toy department?"

"Yes, please," said Gertrude.

Nellie was about to say "No, thank you" when her eye caught sight of a policewoman and a policeman walking between the rows of hanging clothes.

"Quick, Gertrude, quick! Go home," said Nellie. "They might arrest you."

"Me?" said Gertrude. "Arrest me? Whatever for?"

"For being a vandal," said Nellie.

Gertrude was deeply offended. "I am not a vandal, whatever that is. I am a dragon. I'll show them."

She flew into the air and with a graceful glide swooped over the police officers, knocking their hats off, one, two, as she went. She turned and with a flap of her wings disappeared downstairs.

The police officers were not pleased. They picked up their hats and dusted them. Then they took out their notebooks.

"You see?" said the manager. "Someone's

playing tricks. It's most upsetting. We're losing business. And the damage. See for yourselves." The police officers began writing.

"Come on, Nellie" said Dad. "Let's go to the toy department." As there was no sign of Gertrude, Nellie didn't protest. She enjoyed looking at the toys and bought a floppy green-and-yellow frog with her pocket money. On the way out of the shop they passed the sweet counter. Nellie remembered she wanted some toffees, but when she looked there wasn't a toffee in sight.

"Well," said the shop assistant to her friend. "It was like the invisible man. The toffees flew through the air into the bag and the bag went out of the shop."

"What? All by itself?"

"All by itself. That's the honest truth. Seeing is believing. It floated out. I've never seen anything like it."

"Didn't you try to grab it?"

"Grab it? Not me. It gave me the fright of my life."

"Let's go home, Dad," said Nellie.

When they got home, Nellie went down the garden to the old garden shed. She opened the door.

"Hello, Nellie," said Gertrude. "You're too late for a toffee." There was an empty carrier bag on the floor, and toffee papers were all over the shed.

"Do you know you're wanted by the police?" asked Nellie.

"Me? Whatever for?" asked Gertrude.

"For stealing toffees for one thing. It'll probably be on the news. And look at all this evidence."

"What? You mean the toffee papers?" said

Gertrude. "That's easy enough." With a huge breath she sucked up the papers like a vacuum cleaner. Pointing her face towards the door she blew. There was a mighty roar and a stream of flame. Toffee paper ashes floated gently away on the breeze.

"There," said Gertrude. "All gone."

"Really, Gertrude, really, you are the limit," said Nellie.

"Well, what's a few toffees between friends?" said Gertrude.

Nellie let out a huge sigh, shrugged her shoulders and went back indoors. Gertrude lay back on her sacks, licked her lips and smiled a wicked dragon smile.

2 Nellie and the Flying Umbrella

Nellie looked out of the window. It had stopped raining but the wind still blew. She pressed her nose against the glass and blew steam onto the window pane. She moved back and slowly the mist cleared. Before it had all gone Nellie traced an N on the window with her finger.

"Don't do that, Nellie," said Granny May, looking up from her knitting. "The windows were cleaned only the other day. They'll be all smears again at this rate."

Nellie let out a huge sigh.

"Can't you find something to do?"

"I'm bored," said Nellie.

"I know you are. What about doing some clay modelling?"

"Boring."

"Or making some raspberry buns to eat at teatime with Floyd?"

"Boring."

"Nellie," said Granny May, a note of warning in her voice. "Find something to do."

"Can I go out?" At the mention of the word "out", Meg, who had seemed fast asleep in front of the fire, lifted her head and pricked up her ears.

"It's wet outside. What on earth do you want to go out for?" sighed Granny May, already imagining the wet socks and jeans she would be washing and drying when Nellie came in again.

"I want an adventure," said Nellie. "I want to do something brave and bold. I can do it in the garden but I can't do it indoors."

"I should hope not," said Granny May. "This is a living room, not a space ship or anything of that sort." Nellie could tell Granny May was relenting.

"Can I then?"

"Oh, go on. Don't forget to take Meg's ball. That dog's had no exercise all day."

Ball! Yes, she *had* heard aright. Meg was on her feet and barking. She was ready to go out at once.

In the garden Meg jumped around Nellie's feet. She barked and barked for Nellie to throw the ball. Nellie held the solid red ball tightly. She took three paces forward and threw it as hard as she could. It went high over the grass and the vegetable patch and landed somewhere in the wilderness at the bottom of the garden. Meg raced after it. Nellie put her hands over her eyes as Meg ran straight through the middle of Dad's runner beans.

"Heck," Nellie said. When she looked again Meg was nowhere to be seen. "Digging already, I expect," she said.

A sudden gust of wind blew a shower of drips from the lilac tree. They splashed across Nellie's face. She shook herself.

"Dratted wind," she said. "What I need is an umbrella. I'll borrow Granny May's."

Nellie went indoors to fetch the umbrella, remembering just in time to pull off her wellington boots and leave them at the door. She found the umbrella in the cupboard under the stairs and, without asking if she could borrow it, grabbed it, pulled on her boots and was outside again in a jiffy. She opened the umbrella and held it above her head.

"This is more like it," she said. "Now I shan't get wet at all."

The wind whipped under the umbrella and

tried to lift it. Nellie held on tight. Even so she was pulled forward by the gust. Nellie grinned. Holding on was exciting and it had given her an idea. She held tightly to the umbrella with one hand and half climbed the garden wall with the other.

"Floyd!" she yelled. "Floyd!"

After what seemed like ages, Floyd's face appeared at his bedroom window. He looked down at Nellie as she clung to the wall.

"Come on out," Nellie ordered. "I've got this fantastic new game."

Floyd opened his window. "I'm busy just now," he said.

"Doing what?"

"Making some designs."

"This is much better," said Nellie.

"What is?"

"Doing parachute jumping."

"Parachute jumping!" Floyd's eyes lit up. "I'll be right down," he said.

By the time Floyd had clambered into his anorak and found his boots, Nellie was poised on top of the garden wall with the umbrella held aloft. As Floyd came into the garden Nellie cried, "Watch this!"

A gust of wind whipped around Floyd's ears and pushed up under the umbrella. As it did so Nellie jumped into the air and disappeared into her own garden. Floyd clambered up the wall and peered after her. Nellie was in a sprawling heap on the grass.

"Nellie?" Floyd said.

Nellie, who had somehow managed to hang on to the umbrella, looked up and grinned. "That was great," she said. "Want a go?"

Floyd wasn't sure. As Nellie stood up he could see the soggy wet patches on her knees.

"Go on," said Nellie. "Have a go. You've got to wait for the wind. Then, when it gets under the umbrella, you jump. Just like a real parachute. It is. Honest."

"Well . . . " said Floyd.

Nellie thrust the umbrella up at him. "Go on," she said. "It's easy."

The wind blew a sudden blast and before Floyd had the chance to decide whether to jump or not, he was lifted from the wall and carried several paces across the grass before he landed all in a tangle as Nellie had done.

"See!" said Nellie. "See! Parachute jumping!"

Floyd lifted his startled face to Nellie's, who grinned down at him.

"And you didn't let go," she said. Nellie pulled Floyd up and grabbed the umbrella.

"My turn," she said as she hauled herself up the wall. The wind blew. "One, two, three, go!"

yelled Nellie. She jumped from the wall. The wind dropped and she landed with two feet firmly in the flower border. Nellie scrambled out and turned back to survey the damage. One broken plant and two tell-tale footprints. She closed the umbrella.

"I'll get a trowel," she said. "We can tidy it up."

Meg had given up digging in the wilderness and had carried her ball to the garden shed. She dropped it by the door and barked. She put her head to one side and listened. She barked again. A sort of scuffling sound could be heard coming from inside the shed. Meg backed away. The door burst open, followed by a roar of hot air. A bleary-eyed face with two smoking nostrils put

its head outside.

"No," said the half-asleep dragon and the door slammed shut. Meg barked again.

"No," said the voice from inside. "I said no and I mean no." Then, before Meg could even open her mouth, the door was flung open and Gertrude grabbed the ball and flew onto the shed roof with it. Meg looked hopeful.

"Stupid dog," said Gertrude. "What's so fascinating about this silly bit of rubber?" Gertrude began to throw the ball in the air and catch it. Meg wagged her tail. She sat down and waited.

"I may throw it or I may not," said Gertrude. "I may just throw it away."

Meg looked alarmed.

"Or I may eat it." Gertrude poked out her long pink tongue. Meg began to quiver. She barked.

"No barking if you want your ball back," said Gertrude. She was about to balance the ball on her tail when something down the garden caught her attention. Without giving the ball another thought, she dropped it leaving Meg to pounce. Her great wings flapped and lifted her into the air. Nellie was up to something.

Having tidied up the flowerbed, Nellie was poised on the wall, umbrella aloft, ready for another mighty leap.

"Here comes the wind," shouted Floyd.

"One, two, three, go!" shouted Nellie. The wind blew. She jumped. The umbrella soared. Floyd was left staring open-mouthed as Nellie shot skywards. Nellie let out a yell of surprise and tightened her grip on the umbrella handle. It took her a moment or two to realize what was happening. Slowly her ears took in the familiar beating of Gertrude's wings. In a rage she shouted

"Put me down, Gertrude! Put me down!"

"I've got you, Nellie. You're quite safe with me."

"I said put me down!"

There was an ominous ping from the umbrella. It didn't sound as though it was going to last long carrying Nellie's weight high into the air.

"The umbrella's breaking!" shouted Nellie. "Put me down."

"Oh very well," said Gertrude. "If that's what you want, see if I care. I was only trying to be helpful." She dropped down and without another word dumped Nellie on the roof. Nellie wrapped her arms around a chimney pot and clung on as Gertrude flew off in a huff.

Floyd had watched the whole flight with eyes as wide as saucers. Not believing in dragons, he couldn't see Gertrude, so he thought the wind had blown Nellie onto the roof.

"Nellie, Nellie, are you all right?"

Nellie was counting to ten. She wanted to say some really rude things to Gertrude but she also wanted to get down. Gertrude was the only one who could get her down.

"Yes, I'm all right," she called to Floyd. "It's that beastly . . . I mean, kind dragon. She's given me a ride." The kind dragon glided in to land at the other end of the roof. She perched neatly on the roof ridge and began cleaning her claws.

"Gertrude, will you take me down to the garden?" said Nellie. Gertrude ignored her. She carried on with her cleaning as if Nellie wasn't there.

"Please," said Nellie. Gertrude was being incredibly stubborn, Nellie could see that.

"Well, in that case," said Nellie. "I'll have to parachute on my own." She edged her way gingerly to the edge of the roof. It was all she could do to hold onto the umbrella and keep her balance. The wind was getting stronger by the minute. Then an extra strong gust caught the umbrella and with a great whoosh turned it inside out, wrenching it from Nellie's hand.

"Oh, no!" cried Nellie. "Now I'm really stuck." She watched the umbrella spiral in to land on the lawn.

"I'm stuck, Floyd," Nellie shouted. Floyd

could see that. He made up his mind and ran towards the back door.

Then in a voice that only Gertrude could hear Nellie said, "Granny May'll be furious. I won't be allowed out to play for weeks. So, I'm sorry, Gertrude, you won't be able to have any charcoal or raspberry buns or crisps or anything like that because . . . " Nellie didn't have time to finish. Gertrude whisked her from the roof and carried her to the lawn. She even tried to mend the umbrella.

"Oh no," said Nellie. "The umbrella." Gertrude threw it down in disgust.

"It's had it," she said. "Does that mean no raspberry buns?"

Granny May hurried into the garden followed by Floyd.

"Nellie," she said. "Whatever's been going on?" Floyd's anxious face broke into a smile of relief when he saw Nellie.

"How did you get down?" he asked.

"Gertrude lifted me."

"My umbrella!" cried Granny May, picking up the inside-out tangle. "Nellie, how could you?"

"It was an accident," said Nellie.

"It was," said Floyd.

"Indoors at once," said Granny May.

"But . . . " and Nellie shrugged. "Bye,

Floyd."

"Bye, Nellie," said Floyd. He looked around the garden. If there really was a dragon, surely he would see it. As usual there was nothing there. Only Meg carrying her muddy ball down the garden path. Floyd climbed the wall, causing Gertrude to raise a foot to allow him across.

"Only believers see us," she hissed.

Floyd looked over his shoulder. No, nothing there. He jumped into his own garden leaving Gertrude on the wall.

When will Nellie be allowed out again? Gertrude wondered. She hoped Nellie wouldn't have to stay in for too long. She had rather a fancy for a raspberry bun or two.

3 Nellie and the Birthday Surprise

Nellie and Granny May were working hard in the kitchen. Nellie was weighing icing sugar on the kichen scales. Granny May was putting the finishing touches to the large sponge cake she had glued together with strawberry jam.

"Is that right?" Nellie asked. Granny May looked at the scales.

"Exactly right. Well done. You can tip it into the mixing bowl now."

"Can the cake have a rainbow on it?"

"That's a nice idea," said Granny May.

Tomorrow was Floyd's birthday and Nellie and Granny May were making Floyd a surprise birthday cake. There was to be a party in Floyd's garden and all his friends were going to come. Nellie was looking forward to it.

"I hope it doesn't rain," said Nellie.

By lunchtime the cake was finished. Nellie looked at the large round cake in admiration as it sat drying on the kitchen table. Granny May had made a rainbow. Above the rainbow it said "Happy Birthday". Below the rainbow it said "Floyd". Granny May had made a picture of Floyd. Next to the picture was a tiny pair of trainers just like Floyd's. Real icing ones sitting on the cake.

"It's brilliant, Gran," Nellie said.

"I'm glad you like it. I hope Floyd will."

"He will. He'll think it's great. Where are the candles going to go?"

"Where would you like them?"

"Round the edge."

"We'll put them on tomorrow," said Granny May. With great care she lifted the cake and placed it on a shelf in the larder. She closed the larder door. The cake was safe. At least Nellie hoped it was.

Nellie strolled into the garden, the sun warm on her face. When she was sure no one was looking, especially Meg, since Nellie didn't want any noisy barking, she walked down the path to the shed in the wilderness at the bottom of the garden. Very carefully, so as not to make any sound, Nellie peeped in the window. She shaded her face with her hand. Through the gloom she could make out a pile of sacks in the corner. They were rising and falling to the breathing of the dragon who lay asleep underneath them. Nellie crept from the window.

"Good, still asleep," she whispered. "I hope she doesn't wake up until after the party."

Back in the kitchen Nellie checked the larder door was closed and shut the back door properly just in case. Floyd's birthday cake would be the very thing a hungry dragon would eat if she had the chance. There was nothing Gertrude liked more than a nice sticky cake.

When Granny May said it was time to buy

Floyd's birthday present and take Meg to the park, Nellie looked anxiously down the garden.

"I hope Gertrude stays asleep," she sighed.

This was not to be. As Nellie was buying Floyd's birthday present — three packets of the stickers he was saving, — Gertrude's eyelids began to flicker. As Nellie and Granny May were playing ball in the park, Gertrude sighed a long, steamy dragon sigh and stretched, dropping sacks all over the shed floor. She lay there for an hour or two more, dragon-dozing with eyelids half open. By the time it was Nellie's bedtime, Gertrude's tummy gave a long low rumble, causing her eyes to open wide. She jumped up at once, ready for some breakfast.

"Now, what shall it be?" cried Gertrude bursting into the garden. She saw Nellie's bedroom curtains were drawn and that it was getting dark.

"I'll pop up and see if Nellie's got any charcoal before she goes to sleep."

Nellie was already asleep when there was a tap-tapping at her window. Meg lifted her head. She smelt Gertrude and rested her chin on her paws, waiting to see what Nellie would do.

"What's that?" said Nellie, waking up.

"It's me," said Gertrude. "Hurry up."

"Hurry up what?" said Nellie, stumbling out of bed.

"Hurry up and get me some breakfast."

"But it's bedtime," said Nellie pulling back the curtains and opening the window. "I was asleep."

"When a dragon's hungry a dragon has to eat. I need feeding."

"Well, there's nothing I can do about it now," said Nellie. "The barbecue charcoal's locked in the old coal shed. I'm in my pyjamas."

"Some friend you are!"

"It's not my fault if you want breakfast in the middle of the night."

"Huh!" said Gertrude. But she knew Nellie was right.

Nellie went back to bed and Gertrude flew to the vegetable patch. She picked a pile of Dad's broad beans and munched them hungrily one after another, pods and all, until the rumbling in her tummy stopped. With the whole night before her and everyone asleep she decided to do some flying practice. Beating her wings, she launched herself into the dark sky, blowing fire to light her way.

The next day was sunny and bright. When Nellie went into the garden she looked over the garden wall. Floyd's dad was arranging a table on the grass. Nellie waved. She looked down her own garden to the old shed. There was no sign of Gertrude.

"I'll have a look," she said. "Just to make sure." The shed door was open and the shed empty, apart from the sacks which were scattered all over the floor.

"I wonder where she is?" said Nellie. But she didn't have time to wonder for long. Granny May was calling her to come indoors. She wanted Nellie to help make some raspberry buns.

When it was time for the party, Nellie put on her new jeans and trainers. The last thing they did was put the candles on the cake. Nellie counted them carefully. Floyd was seven today. She stuck seven holders into the icing and put a candle into each holder.

"We've got to keep the cake a surprise," said Nellie.

"Don't worry, we will," said Granny May. "Off you go and don't forget Floyd's present."

By the time Gertrude circled down in a graceful glide above Nellie's garden the party was in full swing. The sound of children's voices drifted up to greet her. Gertrude's sharp eyes saw at once the many children running and laughing in Floyd's garden.

"What on earth are they doing? Who are they all?" said Gertrude. She was tired and, as usual, hungry. "All a dragon wants is a little something to eat and some peace and quiet."

Nellie was being the blind man in a game of blind man's bluff. There was a burst of excited voices as she just missed catching someone. Gertrude came in to land on the garden wall.

"This looks like a party," she said. "Oh well, if a dragon can't have peace a dragon must join in."

Nellie was feeling her way across the grass. She didn't know where anyone was. The children around her were quietly tiptoeing away. Gertrude decided to help Nellie out. She swooped and lifting Nellie by the shoulders dropped her on top of a small boy. He let out a cry of surprise and fright.

Nellie knew exactly what had happened. She pulled off her blindfold and looked around her. Gertrude was back on the garden wall. She crooned to Nellie, "His turn now."

The small boy was in no state to take a turn. He was so upset that Granny May had to give him a big cuddle.

"That was too rough, Nellie," said Floyd's dad. "And if you're the blind man you're not supposed to cheat."

"I didn't," said Nellie. By the look on Floyd's dad's face, Nellie could see he didn't believe her.

"Please don't interfere, Gertrude," said Nellie.

"Interfere! Interfere!" said Gertrude. "If that's what you call it, you're on your own, Nellie."

"Good," said Nellie. Gertrude's eyes narrowed and she stuck her nose in the air.

The next game was to be musical chairs. In spite of being in a huff, Gertrude looked on from the corner of her eye as chairs were placed ready for the children to run around. The music began and when it stopped everyone ran for a chair. There was a lot of shouting and shoving until one person was left standing, chairless. They were out. A chair was taken away and the music began again.

"Oh, I like this game," said Gertrude. She hopped from the wall and pushed her way through the running children. Not waiting for the music to stop she sat down. Being a dragon, her bottom was rather large and rather heavy. There was a snapping sound as two of the chairs collapsed and broke. Gertrude ended up on the grass. Nellie helped her up. The music stopped. Everyone stared as Nellie stood amongst the bits of splintered chair.

"Nellie," gasped Granny May.

"It wasn't me," said Nellie. "It was the dragon." The dragon was brushing herself down and looking a little surprised.

"Well, well," she said. "Fancy the chairs collapsing like that." No one but Nellie heard and no one but Nellie saw.

"If you can't play properly, Nellie, you'll have to go home," Granny May said.

"Please, don't join in any more, Gertrude,

please," said Nellie.

"I won't. I won't," said Gertrude. "I'm sorry. Didn't mean to. It was a mistake. It really was." Gertrude crossed the lawn. She stopped and turned. "Only if this is a party, where's the food?"

"I'll bring you some," said Nellie. "Only please stay on the wall. Please."

Gertrude didn't join in any more games. She sat on the wall, her mouth watering, waiting for the food.

"How did you do that trick with the chairs?" asked Floyd. "It was like Kung Fu."

"I didn't. I told you. It was Gertrude."

"Come on, Nellie. If there's a dragon where is she?"

"On the wall." Floyd looked. Gertrude poked her tongue out at him.

"There's nothing there, Nellie. You can't expect me to believe in something that isn't there."

When it was time for tea, Floyd's mum and dad and Granny May carried plates of delicious things from the kitchen and put them on the table. The children crowded round and filled their plates. Gertrude's nose twitched. She couldn't wait. She jumped into the garden and weaved her way to the table. Food suddenly began disappearing in front of everyone's eyes.

First it was a plateful of sausage rolls, gone in a flash. Then it was raspberry buns.

"Oh!" drooled Gertrude, "delicious!" as one after the other she popped them into her mouth. She scooped up a plateful of cucumber sandwiches and ate the whole lot at once.

"Scrumptious," she said, her mouth bursting. "Absolutely scrumptious."

"Gertrude," said Nellie. "Gertrude, stop it!"

"I can't," said Gertrude. "It's bliss." She stuffed a clawful of biscuits into her mouth.

"You're a horrid, greedy dragon. You're spoiling everything."

"What, little old me? Fiddlesticks," said Gertrude, spraying Nellie with chocolate chip cookie crumbs. "I never spoil anything."

At last Gertrude seemed to have eaten enough. The grown-ups were astonished at how quickly everything had gone.

"You keep off the birthday cake," warned Nellie. "If you touch it, I'll never bring you anything to eat ever again."

"I don't want any birthday cake," said Gertrude. "I'm full." But when she saw the cake she changed her mind. It was Nellie who carried the cake from the kitchen.

"Quick, blow out the candles before the wind does, Floyd," shouted Nellie. With an enormous puff, Floyd blew. The seven candles flickered and went out. There was a cheer.

"What a fantastic cake," said Floyd. "That's a picture of me." He stared at the icing trainers. "Can I keep them?" he asked.

"Of course you can," said Granny May. Gently she lifted the icing trainers from the cake and gave them to him. Floyd cut the first slice.

"Don't forget to make a wish," cried Nellie.

Floyd had the first piece and Granny May cut lots more slices. Soon everyone had cake except Gertrude. Watching everyone eat made her want some very badly. There was quite a lot of cake left. Gertrude swooped to the table.

"I'll cut you some," said Nellie, but she was too late. Before everyone's eyes the cake seemed to lift into the air and vanish. It was only Nellie who saw what really happened — Gertrude stuffing the whole lot into her mouth and swallowing it whole.

"You didn't even chew it," said Nellie.

"Didn't need to," said Gertrude.

"You deserve to be sick."

"Sick?" said Gertrude. She patted her tummy. It gurgled. "Me sick? Never." There was more gurgling. "But I do think I need a little lie down. I feel a little heavy all of a sudden," she said faintly.

"Good idea," said Nellie.

Later, when everyone had gone home, Nellie

went to the garden shed. She found Gertrude lying under the sacks.

"I'm feeling a little under the weather," she said. "I can't think why."

"You don't want to admit how greedy you are."

"Me? Greedy?" said Gertrude.

"The best thing you can do is sleep it off," said Nellie.

"Sleep, sleep, yes, I'll go to sleep." Gertrude closed her eyes. As Nellie closed the shed door there was one more loud rumble from Gertrude's tummy.

"Are all dragons as greedy as Gertrude?" Nellie said. "I wonder if they are?"

4 Nellie Goes Swimming

Granny May lay in a deckchair on the lawn, fanning herself with a newspaper.

"Goodness, it's hot," she said.

The sun streamed down from the cloudless blue sky, scorching the lawn and anything else in its gaze. Dad was sitting on the grass, drinking a cup of tea and trying to finish his crossword puzzle. Gertrude lay in the shade of the old apple tree, fast asleep and snoring. Dad and Granny May couldn't hear her. Just as well. The snores were loud. They kept waking up Meg who was trying to sleep under Granny May's deckchair.

Nellie and Floyd were indoors. They were in the front room playing space ships. The room was a shambles. They had turned the chairs and the sofa into a special kind of heap with a hollow in the middle. This was the space ship. Nellie and Floyd were inside the space ship shooting down an attacking enemy. The shooting was noisy. It was so noisy that Granny May could hear it in her deckchair.

"What on earth are those children up to?" she said. Dad grunted. He was working hard on a clue.

"I said, I wonder what on earth those . . . oh, never mind." Granny May settled into her deckchair. The sun was making her sleepy. "You said you were going to take them to the open air pool," she said. Dad grunted again.

"Did you say something?" he asked.

"You said you were going to take Nellie and Floyd swimming in the open air pool."

"Yes, good idea. I will," said Dad. "I'll have a go at one more . . . " He was about to say "clue" but didn't because there was a loud crash inside the house. Meg ran out from under the deckchair barking. Even Gertrude opened an eye.

"I'll go and see what they're up to," said Dad. "And get them ready to go." Dad found Nellie trying to mend the standard lamp. It had been knocked over in a particularly fierce battle.

"Oh, Nellie!" said Dad when he saw it.

"It only needs a bit of glue here and here," said Nellie. "Oh, and here."

"It looks like a write-off to me," said Dad.

"Is it?" said Nellie. She looked glum. "I'm sorry. It was an accident." Both Nellie and Floyd looked downcast. Dad couldn't help smiling.

"Let me see what I can do," he said. "I want this room tickety boo tidy or we don't go swimming, and I want it tidy fast."

Nellie and Floyd rushed to put the furniture back where it belonged. Dad set to work with glue and string and stuck and tied and twisted the string tight. Soon the lamp was whole again. Dad laid it carefully on the carpet.

"Why's it tied up?" said Nellie.

"The string's holding it together until the glue sets," said Dad. "Nobody is to touch it."

"That's very clever," said Floyd, looking at the trussed-up lamp. "Will it be all right?"

"It won't be as good as it was," said Dad. "But with any luck it'll work. No more playing in the front room."

"We won't," said Nellie.

"Swimming things," said Dad.

Floyd ran next door to fetch his trunks and towel. Nellie ran into the garden. Her things were already by the front door.

"We're going swimming," she called. Gertrude opened one eye, then the other.

"Have a nice time," said Granny May, half asleep.

They were going to walk to the pool which wasn't far away. They set off down the pavement. If Nellie had looked behind her she would have seen a hot and half-asleep dragon following them.

"A dragon doesn't like it hot," mumbled Gertrude. "A dragon likes it nice and cool. Where are the clouds in this blue, blue sky?"

When they arrived at the swimming pool, Dad bought the tickets and he, Nellie and Floyd went through the turnstile. They could hear the cries of the people already playing and swimming in the water.

"I want to jump off the springboard," said Nellie.

"So do I," said Floyd. They hurried to get changed.

When Gertrude arrived at the turnstile, try as she might, she couldn't squeeze through it.

"Drat it," she said. "I'll have to fly." Hot though she was, she spread her wings and with some effort launched herself skywards. Up she flew, over the entrance, across the fence until she was hovering high above the cool, blue water.

"Here goes," she said. Without a moment's thought for those already in the pool she dived. The people in the pool were astonished by a terrific splash. It caused an enormous wave which rushed to the side of the pool, spilling over the edge and drenching the people standing nearby.

"Who did that?" demanded the pool attendant. He looked into the water at the surprised swimmers. Gertrude surfaced, a smile of relief on her face. She was cool at last.

"Come on, own up. Who made that big splash?" he said again.

"Little old me," said Gertrude with a dragon grin. "I enjoyed making it so much I'm going to make another one." She spread her wings above the water and took off. Up she flew.

"What's going on?" asked Dad as he, Nellie and Floyd came out of the changing rooms.

"Someone's made a big splash. So big the water level's gone down," a woman told them.

"Who would do a thing like that?" said Dad.

Nellie's eye was caught by the sight of something hovering high above them. It glinted gold in the sunlight.

"Oh, no! Watch out! It's Gertrude," she said. Gertrude plunged for her second dive. There was another monster splash as Gertrude hit the water. Spray flew into the air and another great wave pounded up and over the sides of the pool. The attendant was furious. The water in the pool went even lower.

"Who is doing this?" he bellowed.

"I've already told you," smirked Gertrude. "Little old me."

"Gertrude!" shouted Nellie. "You're not to

44

do it again. You're emptying the pool."

"Don't be an old meany boots, Nellie."

"Look at the water level," said Nellie. Gertrude looked. Certainly, it was a long way below the mark on the wall where it should have been.

"Did I do that?" Gertrude asked.

"Yes, you did," said Nellie.

Gertrude put her hand to her mouth. "Oh, dear," she chuckled. "I'll do floating instead."

"Good," said Nellie.

The attendant waited. There were no more giant splashes. The people who had got out of the water in a fright got back in again.

But Gertrude now became a problem in the middle of the pool. People couldn't see her so they kept bumping into her. It didn't worry Gertrude very much. If she saw them coming she pushed them away, if she didn't they bumped her. Gertrude hardly felt the bump.

Unfortunately the swimmers did. Dragon scales are hard. One bruise on the head is bad enough but two or three can give you a nasty headache.

"Don't be ridiculous," said the pool attendant when the complaints reached him. "There can't possibly be an invisible object in the middle of the pool."

"But there is," said the swimmers. They showed the attendant their bumps and bruises.

Dad, Nellie and Floyd were having a lovely time. They were quite unaware of the problem in the middle of the pool. That is until the attendant blew his whistle and told everyone to get out of the water.

"At last," said Gertrude. "A bit of peace and quiet." She settled herself comfortably on her back and paddled round in circles.

The swimmers gathered round the attendant. "It has been reported to me," he said, "that there is, and I hesitate to say it for fear of seeming foolish, an invisible object in the middle of the pool. This being the case, I wish you all to stay here while I investigate this phenomenon myself. Thank you." The swimmers applauded his bravery.

"Oh, no," said Nellie. "Gertrude," she called. "Gertrude." Gertrude didn't hear. She had dozed off.

The attendant went to the edge of the pool

and dived in. He swam this way, he swam that. He zigzagged up and down. He was almost ready to give up when bang, he collided with the object. The object woke up.

"Do you mind?" it said. The attendant didn't hear. He was rubbing the bruise on his head. He stretched out his hand and felt something hard and scaly. He was astonished.

"Oh, don't," said Gertrude. "You're tickling." She wriggled away, disturbing the water and adding to the consternation of the attendant who couldn't see any reason for the disturbance. He moved forward and stretched out his hand. His fingers wriggled under Gertrude's armpit. Gertrude burst into giggles.

"Oh, don't!" she said. "Don't!"

"Gertrude," called Nellie. "I think you should get out of the water."

"Why?"

"Because . . . " Nellie thought quickly. "Because you didn't pay for a ticket."

Gertrude couldn't deny this, and as she was delightfully cool, she decided to do what Nellie asked. She swam to the side causing more unexplained splashings and climbed out. She shook herself and went to lie on the grass.

"Why don't you lie on the changing room roof?" suggested Nellie. "Then people won't keep falling over you. You'll have peace and quiet there."

"Good idea," said Gertrude and she flew to the roof where she settled herself down for a quiet doze. "Thank goodness for that," said Nellie.

The attendant gave up his search for the invisible object. He had tried and tried to find it again but whatever it was had gone.

"It's safe to swim now," he shouted to the waiting swimmers. The swimmers gave a cheer and got back in the water. Soon the pool was back to normal. The attendant kept a look-out for further trouble but there was none.

When Dad said it was time to go Nellie and Floyd groaned.

"Must we?" they said.

"Yes," said Dad. "But you can each have an ice cream to eat on the way home."

"Yummy," cried Nellie and was the first to get her clothes on.

"We're going now, Gertrude," Nellie called. The sleepy dragon waved and followed them.

As Nellie, Floyd and Dad went into the ice cream shop, Gertrude looked in the window to see what they were buying. She banged on the glass. Everyone turned, startled, including the shopkeeper. It was only Nellie who saw who it was.

"I want one too," said Gertrude. "A

chocolate one."

The shopkeeper went outside to see who had banged but, of course, he saw no one there.

"Stop creating a disturbance," said Nellie. "I'll get you one with my pocket money."

"You are kind," crooned Gertrude. "So kind."

Dad bought them each an ice cream and Nellie bought another one, with her pocket money.

"Are you sure you can eat two?" asked Dad.

"It's not for me, it's for the dragon," said Nellie.

"I see," said Dad. Floyd didn't say anything. Outside the shop Gertrude pounced.

"Which is mine?" she asked.

"This one," said Nellie.

"Thank you very much, Nellie," Gertrude said and flew onto a lamp-post. She wrapped her pink tongue round the cool chocolate ice cream and sucked. It was delicious.

"Mmm," sighed Gertrude. "Scrummy scrumptious."

"You haven't eaten it already, have you?" said Dad when he saw Nellie only had one ice cream left.

"I gave to to Gertrude," said Nellie. Dad and Floyd looked about them. There was no dragon and no ice cream to be seen.

"Where is she then?" Dad asked.

"On top of the lamp-post," said Nellie.

Dad and Floyd looked up. Gertrude looked down. She was licking the last of the ice cream from her claws.

"Yah boo sucks to you," she said rudely. Then raising her hands to her head pulled the most horrible face.

"Oh, really," said Nellie and walked off down the pavement. Not seeing anything at all, Dad and Floyd followed her.

Gertrude flew from her lamp-post and followed along behind. She pulled a series of even more horrible faces calling "Yah boo sucks to you" all the way home. Nellie ignored her.

Really, Gertrude could be very trying sometimes.

When they got home Granny May took out one of her special home-made cakes for tea. Nellie took Gertrude a slice. Gertrude was really pleased and promised to be good for the rest of the day.

"Well, that's something," sighed Nellie, even though there wasn't much of the day left.

5 Nellie and the Tree Den

Nellie ran into the garden. It had been raining for days and days but today the sun was shining. Meg carried her pulley toy, the floppy rubber triangle Granny May had bought at the pet shop. She shook it and shook it and as she shook she growled horribly.

"Who is the fiercest dog in the world?" said Nellie, getting hold of the pulley toy hanging from Meg's mouth. Meg growled and pulled hard. Nellie pulled hard too. They pulled each other backwards and forwards across the lawn.

Floyd's head appeared above the garden wall.

"I might have known," he said. "What a row you two make."

"It's not me," said Nellie, letting go of the pulley toy. "It's Meg." Meg ran across the lawn shaking her head and growling as fiercely as ever.

"That dog's barmy," said Floyd.

"No, she's not," said Nellie. "She's just being a dog and that's what dogs do."

"Waste of time if you ask me," said Floyd.

"Not if you're a dog," said Nellie.

"Do you want to play?" asked Floyd.

"Don't mind," said Nellie. "What?" Floyd thought for a minute.

"Being on a desert island?"

"No," said Nellie. She didn't like that idea. Her eyes travelled down the garden to the old apple tree.

"We could try and make a swing."

"What, and hang it on that old tree?" said Floyd.

"Yes. Why not?" Floyd looked doubtful.

"Well . . . " he began.

"I've got it. I've got it," cried Nellie. "Even better. A tree den and you have to climb a ladder to get to it."

"Well," said Floyd. "I dunno."

"We could play at being on a desert island and we have to build the tree den to protect us from all the fierce animals that might eat us up," said Nellie.

"Yes," said Floyd. "But we'd need wood and tools and nails and things."

"Come on over," said Nellie. "Let's make some plans."

When Dad and Granny May stood in the garden and surveyed the old apple tree, Nellie hopped from foot to foot in excitement.

"We could do it, couldn't we?" said Nellie. "The tree's not too high or anything."

"I don't see why not," said Dad. "As long as we make sure the floor is firm and safe and the walls are strong."

"What are we going to use for wood?" asked Granny May. "There are those spare bits in the old coal shed. Will they be enough?"

"Possibly," said Dad. "Why don't we pull down the old garden shed? We never use it and it is an eyesore."

"No," gasped Nellie. "No, you can't do that."

"Why ever not?" said Dad.

"Because Gertrude lives in it."

Gertrude had been dozing in a patch of the sun in the wilderness until her sharp ears had picked up the words "garden shed". She stood up and followed the conversation intently.

"Oh, come on, Nellie," said Floyd. "You're always kidding on about this dragon but no one ever sees her."

"I do."

"Yes, you do. So you say." Something pinched Floyd's leg. "Ouch," he said and rubbed it.

If Floyd could have seen what Nellie could see it would have been an outraged dragon. A dragon who was about to pinch his other leg should he utter another word against her.

"No," said Nellie. "No, if it means pulling the shed down to build a tree den, then I don't want one."

"Thank you, Nellie," said Gertrude. "How kind. I'll remember that."

"All right, all right," said Dad. "We'll worry about the shed later. Let's use the wood we already have and if there's enough we can leave the shed where it is."

"So it's wood you want is it?" said Gertrude. "I'm sure I can manage to find you some bits and pieces. But first I must start my campaign."

"What campaign?" asked Nellie.

"The Save Gertrude's Garden Shed campaign. Paper and paint if you please, Nellie."

"But, Gertrude, are you sure this is a good idea?"

"Of course. Dragonpower and all that. A dragon has to stand up for her rights. My rights are a garden shed to myself. A roof over my head. A sack or two to lie myself upon. Simple needs but essential for dragon comfort."

"I'll fetch you some," said Nellie.

"Bright colours, please," said Gertrude.

As the sawing and hammering began near the old apple tree, so did the painting of slogans on paper at the far end of the garden by the shed. By the time Dad and Granny May were fitting the floor of the tree den into the apple tree, Gertrude had finished the first stage of her campaign. It was Floyd who noticed the shed first.

"Look at that," he said. "Nellie, did you do it?"

Granny May, Dad and Nellie turned to look. The shed was covered from top to bottom in posters. "Save my shed" said one. "A dragon's right to a roof," said another.

"A dragon lives here," read Granny May.

"Dragons are people the same as anyone else," read Dad. "Goodness, Nellie, you needn't have worried," he said. "We can buy some more wood if we need it. We won't knock the shed down."

"It wasn't me," said Nellie.

"It *wasn't* you," said Granny May, puzzled. "You've been here all the time."

"It was somebody," said Dad, firmly. "But

not a dragon, of that I am certain."

Gertrude came skipping along the wall, pleased with her efforts. "What do you think, Nellie?" she asked.

"Very good," said Nellie. "They know it wasn't me but they don't believe it was you."

"What more can a dragon do?" said Gertrude, raising her eyes to the blue sky. "The knights of old believed in us. What about St George and all that? What's the matter with these modern folk? Shall I give them a surprise and burn down the apple tree?"

"No," said Nellie. "Don't you dare."

"Only joking. I'm off to fetch wood. There's some dumped in a skip down the road."

"Thanks, Gertrude," called Nellie.

The floor of the tree den was nearly finished when the first of the wood arrived. Six long planks landed on the grass with a crash. Before Nellie could stop her Gertrude was off to fetch more.

"Where on earth did that come from?" said Dad.

"It seemed to come from out of the sky," said Floyd.

"Now don't you start, Floyd," said Granny May. "It's enough with Nellie's imaginings. All the same this is a puzzle."

The next load of wood arrived when they

were having a tea break. Nellie ran into the garden when she saw Gertrude drop an old table top on the grass.

"Here," Nellie said. "Have a chocolate biscuit, Gertrude."

"Yummy, thanks," said Gertrude.

"And really that's enough."

"Just one more load," said Gertrude. "I'm not taking any chances with my shed." And off she flew. Nellie looked at the growing pile of wood on the grass.

"There's much too much," she said. "But we could have a bonfire and make baked potatoes. We could eat them in the tree den when we get it finished." Pleased with this idea she ran back indoors to finish her drink.

By the end of the day the tree den had a floor and walls but no roof. Dad said, "Nellie and Floyd can put the roof on tomorrow with a bit of help from us." He was bemused by the great pile of wood. He wondered if Floyd's dad had dropped it over the wall. "I must remember to ask him," he said. They went indoors happy with what they had done.

The next day was lovely and sunny. When Nellie looked out of her bedroom window she saw more posters on the garden shed. One said, "Keep the shed, keep the dragon." Another said, "Long live dragons and they do." One that

Nellie particularly liked said, "What is a dragon without her shed, a little lost creature with no place for her head." Then Nellie looked at the tree den. It wouldn't take long to put the roof on and dad said he was going to make a wooden ladder now there was so much wood.

"Yippee!" cried Nellie. "Our very own tree den."

"Woof," said Meg joining in. "Woof, woof."

When they had finished breakfast, Nellie, Dad, Granny May and Meg went into the garden. Floyd came over the wall to join them. The sawing and hammering began. It woke Gertrude.

"Oh," she said. "They're up. I must ask Nellie what she thinks about my posters." Her eyes narrowed. "If anyone touches my shed, I'll sizzle 'em." She took a deep breath, opened the shed door and blew. Orange flame roared through the doorway, singeing the wooden door frame. Gertrude took another deep breath and blew. "I'll sizzle 'em to bits." Sparks flew through the air. One caught the edge of a poster and settled there glowing. Not noticing the effect of her flame throwing, Gertrude flew onto the garden wall and skipped along it to say "Hello" to Nellie.

"Hello," said Nellie looking up. Her eyes caught sight of smoke coming from the end of the garden. "Where's the smoke coming from?" she asked. Gertrude turned to look.

"My shed," she gasped. "My beloved shed. It's on fire!"

"Quick, everyone," said Nellie. "The shed's on fire." Nellie ran for the garden hose.

"Save my shed. Save my shed," moaned Gertrude from the garden wall.

Nellie pointed the hose at the flames creeping up the doorpost. Dad turned on the water. There was a great deal of hissing as the flames went out.

"Not much damage," said Nellie. The doorpost was a bit charred but the door still worked.

"Gertrude, you must be more careful. Breathing fire is all very well but it *is* dangerous."

Gertrude went straight into the shed and painted another poster. It said, "No smoking, No flaming, No sizzling. By order." She hung it on the wall.

"Well, just so long as you remember," said Nellie.

"I will," said Gertrude. She chewed a claw. "What a silly me."

"Not much damage," said Dad looking in. "I wonder how that started? The dragon breathing fire, eh?" He grinned, teasing her. Nellie didn't say anything.

When the last nail was hammered into the roof and the ladder had been nailed to the tree, the tree den was declared finished. Nellie and Floyd climbed up and sat inside it. There was a

window on the side to look out from and they could see through the doorway too.

"It could be a pirate ship," said Floyd.

"It could be a space ship," said Nellie.

"It can be anything you like," said Granny May. Meg put her feet on the bottom rung of the ladder and looked up.

"Not for dogs," said Granny May and stroked Meg's ears.

Gertrude flew onto the roof of the tree den. She curled her neck down and looked in the window.

"What about some baked potatoes?" she asked. "If you fetch the potatoes I could get a bonfire started with all this leftover wood."

Nellie laughed. "I had the same idea too," she said.

When the bonfire was made, Dad struck a match and lit the newspaper underneath. Gertrude blew a gentle stream of flame into the wood to help it along. Dad was pleased with how easily the bonfire caught alight. He didn't know Gertrude was helping. He thought he had done it all by himself. Gertrude kept blowing. When Nellie came, carrying a large bag of potatoes from indoors, Gertrude said,

"I've made embers. Put them there." Nellie laid the potatoes on the embers and Gertrude prodded them into place with her claws.

When the potatoes were done, Nellie and Floyd ate two each in the tree den. They pretended they were on a desert island, shipwrecked after a storm. They were the only ones saved and the tree den was keeping them safe.

Gertrude lined her potatoes up along the wall. There were ten. She ate them one after another.

"Absolutely scrummy," she said when she'd finished. She licked her claws. "Just off for a doze," she called to Nellie. And doze she did, tucked up under her sacks in the old garden shed.

6 Nellie and the Mystery Box

Granny May had been rummaging in the attic all morning. She made lots of bangs and thumps on the ceiling in Nellie's room. Meg kept jumping up and growling. They were not the kind of noises she was used to and she didn't like them.

"It's all right, Meg," said Nellie. "It's Granny May doing things in the attic."

"What things?" said a voice from the window.

"Hello, Gertrude," said Nellie.

"Well, what things is she doing? I want to know," said Gertrude. She was leaning over from the roof to look in Nellie's window. Her

face was upside down.

"I don't know," said Nellie.

"Go and look then. It might be something interesting."

"Gertrude, don't you think you should be careful. You might fall off the roof," said Nellie.

"A dragon wants to know what a dragon wants to know."

"Oh, all right," said Nellie. She went to the foot of the ladder on the landing and called up, "How are you doing up there?"

There was no reply but there was a loud thump. The ladder rattled. Gingerly Nellie began to climb it. As her head went through the trap door, she smelt the dry, musty smell of the attic. It had a muffled warm feeling to it.

Granny May was on the far side doing something with what looked like a box.

"How are you doing, Granny May?" called Nellie. The unexpected voice startled Granny May. She looked up quickly.

"Oh, Nellie," she said. "You be careful on that ladder now."

"What are you doing?" said Nellie.

Granny May rubbed a grubby hand across her face, leaving a dirty streak on her forehead.

"Having a good clear up," she said. "I've found something that I think might interest you. I'd forgotten all about it."

"What is it?" said Nellie.

"You wait and see. I've nearly finished. I'll bring it down when I come." Granny May moved a pile of old newspapers. She dropped them by the trapdoor. A cloud of dust exploded into the air. Nellie wrinkled up her nose.

"Why anyone bothered to save those papers I'll never know," said Granny May. "A load of clutter, that's what they are."

"Are you coming down now?" Nellie asked, wanting to know what Granny May had found.

"Soon," came the reply.

Nellie knew that was that and she'd have to wait. She went back down the ladder and into her room. Gertrude was still hanging from the roof.

"Did you find out?" she said crossly. "You took long enough."

"She's clearing out the attic, I think," said Nellie.

"You think!" said Gertrude.

"And she's found something that might interest me," Nellie said.

Gertrude somersaulted from the roof onto the window-sill. "What?"

"I don't know, she wouldn't say," said Nellie.

"Didn't you ask her?"

"I did and she said I'd have to wait and see."

"Wait and see. Wait and see. I want to know *now*. A dragon doesn't like to be kept waiting," said Gertrude. Nellie could see Gertrude's nose tilting up and knew she was getting huffy.

"She said she'd be down soon," said Nellie.

There was a terrific bang and thud on the landing. Meg barked. Nellie ran to the landing to see what had happened. Granny May was on her way down the ladder, steadying a large wooden box.

"Sorry if I startled you," she said . "I dropped the rubbish down. Can you give me a hand with this box?"

Granny May lowered the box down and Nellie stood at the bottom of the steps to steady it. It was large. As Granny May came down the steps, Nellie could feel by the weight of it that it was heavy. When the box finally rested on the landing floor, Nellie pulled it across the carpet and out of the way. Granny May lowered the trapdoor and took down the ladder.

"That's one good job done," she said. "Mind you don't fall over the rubbish. I'll get rid of that first."

Granny May went downstairs with the rubbish. Nellie studied the box. It was very dirty. Underneath all the dirt it looked old. It was big enough to get into. Nellie began to fumble with the catch when an angry voice from her bedroom window reminded her that Gertrude wanted to know what was going on. Gertrude tried to squeeze herself through the window.

"If you don't tell me what the something interesting is I shall break the window and get in and find out for myself," Gertrude yelled.

"It's a box," said Nellie. "A big box and it's heavy. It's on the landing. That's all I know so far."

"A measly box," said Gertrude. "Is that all?"

"I expect the something interesting is inside it."

"Well, don't just stand there," said Gertrude. "Open it."

"Don't be so impatient," said Nellie. "I've got to wait for Granny May, so you'll just have to wait as well."

"Huh!" said Gertrude. She flew down to the garden wall and stood tapping her foot and tut-tutting to herself.

Nellie heard the front door close with a bang and Granny May's footsteps on the stairs.

"Right," said Granny May. "We'll bump the box down the stairs and carry it into the garden. It needs a jolly good clean."

"What's inside?" asked Nellie.

"A surprise," said Granny May.

Nellie was excited. As they bumped the box downstairs and heaved it into the garden, Nellie tried to imagine what could be in it. Treasure, books, toys? Whatever could it be?

As soon as the box was in the garden

Gertrude hurried from the wall to look. She was in such a rush she tripped over Meg and bumped into Granny May. Granny May went backwards and ended up sitting on the box.

"Get off the box," shouted Gertrude rudely. "I want to look." Luckily Granny May couldn't hear her. Instead she turned to Nellie with a curious expression on her face.

"Did you push me?" she asked.

"Of course I didn't," said Nellie. "Are you all right?" Granny May nodded.

"Before we open the box I think we should brush the dust off," she said. Nellie ran to fetch the brush while Granny May pulled the box a little further into the garden. Gertrude hopped from one foot to the other. She wanted the box opened, not cleaned. Nellie came back with the brush and began to brush the box. Clouds of dust rose into the air. It set everyone sneezing.

"There's a key to this somewhere," Granny May said. "You get it nice and clean and I'll try and find it."

"A key! A key!" cried Gertrude. "I haven't time to wait for a key!" She rattled the lid of the box. It didn't budge. She kicked it.

"Ouch!" she cried and held her toe.

"Serves you right," said Nellie.

When Granny May came back with the key Gertrude shouted, "At last and about time too."

"Go on, Nellie, you unlock it," said Granny May, giving Nellie the key. Nellie put the key in the lock and turned it. The catch fell open. Carefully Nellie lifted the lid. Inside the box were lots of folded clothes.

"Clothes," said Gertrude in disgust. "It's old clothes. Really boring. Not in the slightest bit interesting, if you ask me."

"It's dressing-up clothes, Nellie. I used to have such fun with these clothes when I was a little girl," said Granny May.

"Dressing-up and pretend clothes?" said Nellie. "Can I look?"

"Of course you can," said Granny May. "I'm going indoors to clean up. Why don't you ask Floyd to come and play dressing up with you?"

"Dressing-up clothes, eh?" said Gertrude.

"I thought you said it was boring," said

Nellie.

"Well . . ." said Gertrude.

Nellie looked through the box. As well as shirts and dresses and trousers there were hats and gloves and belts and shoes. They were funny, old-fashioned clothes.

"Cor," said Nellie. "I'm going to get Floyd. I bet he'll love this lot." Nellie ran to the garden wall and clambered over.

"Pooh!" said Gertrude. "They smell of moth balls." Nevertheless she began to rummage in the box. She pulled out an old black stole which had long dangling bits on it.

"Oh, locely," said Gertrude. "Hair." She hung the stole over her head. Next she found an old evening dress. It was green and black with large flowers on it.

"Beautiful dress," she said. She tried pulling it over her head but it wouldn't go. Without another thought she tore down the front with a claw and struggled into it as if it were a blouse, first one arm then the other. She took out a pair of red shoes, took one look at her dragon feet and dropped them.

"Hopeless. Too small," she said. "Ah, what's this?" Gertrude pulled out a cloak. "Oooh! Nice skirt," she crowed. This she wrapped around her waist. From somewhere near the bottom of the box she found a safety pin.

"If I can make this work," she said, "I'll have clothes on." Somehow she pinned the cloak so that it stayed together. "A hat. That's what I need next."

Clothes were flung all over the place as Gertrude looked for a suitable hat. "Ah!" she said with a satisfied smile. "A hat!" It was a bright red hat with a floppy brim. Gertrude pulled it down over her ears. It felt most becoming.

"What do I look like? I must know," she said. She skipped to the kitchen window and caught sight of her reflection in the glass. If she'd been a cat she would have purred she was so pleased.

"How handsome I am," she cried. She twirled

in front of the window, her black hair swirling down her back, her hat brim bouncing on her shoulders.

Meg barked. She was startled by Gertrude's odd appearance. A dressed-up dragon was quite an extrordinary sight.

Nellie was the first to climb back over the wall. When she saw Gertrude she gasped. She wanted to laugh but knew Gertrude would be offended so she sat on the wall and stared. Floyd clambered up beside her.

"Crumbs," he said. "Who's that?" Nellie turned to him, surprised.

"Can you see her? It's Gertrude."

"Never," said Floyd. "It's Granny May dressed up. I can tell." Floyd couldn't see the dragon but he could see the clothes. He hadn't looked closely enough to notice that he couldn't see hands or feet. Gertrude's face was covered by the hat brim. Floyd thought it was Granny May. As far as he was concerned there was no one else it could be.

"Your gran's a real sport, isn't she?" he said with a grin.

"But it's not . . . " Nellie didn't finish for Gertrude had just completed another flowing turn when she came face to face with Granny May at the kitchen window. Granny May gave a terrified scream and dropped the pile of dishes she was carrying into the sink. They landed with a crash.

"Eeek!" gasped Gertrude. The crash gave her a horrible fright. She turned and fled down the garden to the safety of her shed, bits of clothing falling from her as she ran.

Granny May's shocked white face stared out of the kitchen window. Nellie ran into the kitchen and Floyd stared in disbelief at the clothes falling all over the garden. Nellie helped Granny May to a chair.

"Goodness, Nellie, you gave me a fright," she said. "I thought I'd seen a ghost. How very clever of you to make a giant puppet like that. You and Floyd have been busy. I just wish you'd warned me, that's all."

Nellie didn't know what to say. The best thing she could manage was "Sorry". This seemed to calm Granny May down a little.

"What a silly I am," said Granny May. "Must be getting old." Floyd poked his head round the door.

"I've collected the clothes from the invisible dragon," he said. Then he grinned. "That was very clever, Granny May."

"Yes," said Granny May. "I thought so too. Well done, both of you." Floyd looked puzzled for a moment. Then he shrugged.

"I'm going to have a go at dressing up in

these," he said, holding up a pair of enormous boots.

Leaving Granny May in the kitchen and Floyd dressing himself up as a pirate, Nellie went down the garden to the old shed. She grinned when she saw Gertrude.

"Are you all right?" she asked. Gertrude was sitting on her sacks, her hair and hat the only items of her dressing-up clothes still in place. She did look, well, just a little bit funny.

"I don't know why you're laughing," she said. "This dragon nearly had a heart attack."

"But is this dragon all right now?"

"She is, thank you," nodded Gertrude, making the brim on her hat sway up and down.

"And so is Granny May, I'm pleased to say. You gave each other a fright."

"You're telling me," said Gertrude.

"So no more dressing up in public," said Nellie

"Oh, all right. Can I keep my hair and hat?" Nellie smiled.

"Of course you can."

Gertrude took off the hair and hat and Nellie hung them on the nail for her. Covering herself with a sack or two Gertrude lay down to recover. Nellie, smiling, closed the door quietly on her way out.

7 Nellie and the Uncatchable Hat

It was a windy day. Leaves were blowing along the pavement and rising in whirls with each strong gust. Nellie, Floyd and Meg were going to the park to play. Granny May came with them as far as the gate. She had her wheeled shopping basket with her, as she was going to do some shopping. Granny May gave Nellie a kiss.

"Off you go," she said. "And don't get up to mischief."

"We won't," said Nellie. She unclipped Meg's lead and threw the ball along the path. Meg ran after it.

"What shall we do first, Floyd?" Nellie asked.
"Feed the ducks?"

"Yes, let's," said Nellie.

The wind was blowing hard enough to make waves on the lake. They had to shout in order to hear each other. Floyd tried to open the bag with the bread in. The wind blew the bag against his chest. In the end he and Nellie made a windbreak with their bodies so that they could get their hands in the bag.

The ducks were hungry. They paddled over to be fed. The wind blew under their feathers and ruffled them.

"Not much fun for ducks in this weather," Nellie shouted, trying to throw bread into the water. Some she managed and some she didn't. The wind kept whipping it back onto the grass. Nellie and Floyd kept picking it up and trying to throw it into the water. However hard they threw, the wind blew the bread back at them.

"The bread's too light," cried Floyd.

"I wouldn't want to eat it if it were heavier," said Nellie.

Meg came trotting up with her ball. She dropped it at Nellie's feet and barked. She wanted it thrown at once. Nellie picked it up and with a mighty throw sent it spinning across the grass.

"Watch out! Here's trouble," said Floyd. It was the park keeper. He looked his usual grumpy self. Nellie smiled.

"Hello," she said.

"Keep that dog under control," said the park keeper. "I don't want it spoiling my flower beds."

"Meg never ever goes on the flowerbeds," said Nellie.

"Never ever," said Floyd, backing her up. The park keeper looked from one to another.

"Just you make sure that she doesn't never ever, that's all."

There was a terrific gust of wind. The distracted park keeper only just got his hand to his hat in time. It nearly blew off.

"Blooming weather," he said and tramped off.

"He's in a bad mood," said Nellie.

"What's new?" said Floyd. He threw the empty paper bag into the rubbish bin. "Race you to the swings." They arrived at the swings quite out of breath. They each jumped on a swing and stopped the wind blowing it higgledy piggledy like a twisting snake.

"What would you do if you saw a snake?" said Nellie.

"Pick it up and eat it! What do you think?" said Floyd.

"Yuk," said Nellie. "And to think you're my friend."

Meg put her ball at the bottom of a tree and started to dig.

"Better not let the park keeper catch Meg doing that," said Floyd.

"Where is he?" said Nellie looking round.

"In the flower garden," said Floyd. "I can see his hat over the hedge." Nellie began swinging.

"Let's see who can go highest," she said.

"I can."

"No, you can't," said Nellie.

They swung as hard as they could. Higher and higher they went. It was made all the more exciting by the wind which buffeted them as they went up and down. They were beginning to slow down when the wind blew with a terrific roar which bent the trees before it. Across the hedge by the flower garden came the park keeper's hat. It was Nellie who saw it.

"Look, Floyd, look! Old grumpy boots has lost his hat."

"Come on, Nellie," said Floyd. "Let's get it."

They jumped from the swings and ran for the hat. The wind was too quick for them. It picked up the hat and blew it across the grass. They ran after it laughing. The park keeper came running behind them. He wasn't laughing. There was a lull in the wind. The hat rested on the grass and Nellie and Floyd nearly caught it when out of the sky swooped a green-and-gold dragon. With a neat flick of the wrist she scooped up the hat and carried it off.

"Oh, no!" groaned the park keeper.

"Typical," said Nellie.

"But the wind wasn't blowing that hard then," said Floyd. It was only Nellie who had seen the dragon and the dragon was, of course, Gertrude. Nellie wondered if Gertrude was going to give the hat back.

The park keeper followed the hat skywards with anxious eyes. So as to be really impressive Gertrude turned a few somersaults. Over and over went the dragon and over and over went the hat.

"Give it back, Gertrude," shouted Nellie.

"Who wants it?" shouted Gertrude.

"You know perfectly well who wants it. Don't

be so mean."

"What do you mean, 'mean'? A dragon is never mean." Gertrude swooped down until the hat was in front of the park keeper, an arm's stretch away. He jumped to get it. Gertrude was too quick for him and as the wind blew she tumbled the hat through the air. The park keeper ran after it. Gertrude was enjoying herself. She was being really wicked.

"The best thing to do is ignore her. If you take no notice she'll stop," said Nellie. "Poor old grumble boots. He'll be exhausted by the time Gertrude's finished."

The park keeper, not knowing he was being teased by a dragon, ran hither and thither after his hat. At one point he half climbed a tree to reach it when it seemed stuck on a branch.

When he nearly had it in his hand the hat disappeared in front of his eyes. In the end he sat on a bench and ran his fingers through his hair in despair.

"My best hat," he said. "The one that keeps my ears warm. Gone. Gone. This blooming wind. Playing tricks. My hat. Now it's gone."

Nellie felt sorry for him. She was cross, very cross with Gertrude. Nellie thought she was being horrid. Gertrude flew down and hovered behind the bench. Nellie ran to her.

"Give the hat back, Gertrude," she said.

"I will, I will. A dragon does everything when a dragon is ready," said Gertrude.

The wind gusted and Gertrude bounced the hat in front of the park keeper and up in the air. He saw it, relief in his face. He jumped up and ran after it. Gertrude bounced the hat up and down, to this side and that. The park keeper jumped and stretched to this side and that, but the hat was always just out of reach. The wind blew and blew.

Floyd thought it a great joke. "You'd think he'd have caught it by now," he said. "Shall we help?"

"It wouldn't do any good," said Nellie. "If only he'd stop running after it she'd lose interest and stop teasing him."

Gertrude, who hadn't enjoyed herself so

much for ages, was flying backwards, a difficult manoeuvre. The park keeper jumped and stretched but still he missed the hat. Gertrude was giggling like anything and not looking where she was going. So it was not surprising that she hit the large oak tree that stood in the middle of the park. This she did, at full speed, bang wallop. Her head jerked back into the hard wood of the tree.

Gertrude groaned, saw stars and slid to the ground where she lay limp and still. The hat rolled across the grass. With a triumphant cry the park keeper dived forward and grabbed it. He picked it up and shook it as if it was a naughty dog. He pulled it onto his head and marched back to his flower garden with hot, red cheeks but well satisfied.

Nellie raced to where Gertrude lay.

"Gertrude," she said. "Gertrude, are you all right?"

Gertrude was not all right. Nellie put her hand on Gertrude's heart. She could feel it beat. She saw the rise and fall of Gertrude's chest as she breathed.

"Thank goodness," she said. Meg snuffled her nose into Gertrude's ear. "She's not dead," Nellie told Meg. Meg whined and sniffed Gertrude until she found the large bump that was growing on Gertrude's head. Very gently she licked it.

"That's enough, Meg," said Nellie. Meg stopped licking and as she did so a trickle of orange dragon blood ran down Gertrude's neck. Nellie took out her handkerchief.

"A cold compress is what we need." She ran to the lake and dipped the hankerchief in the water. She ran back and laid it over Gertrude's bump.

"She's knocked herself out," said Nellie. "We'll have to wait for her to come round." Nellie sat next to Gertrude and held her clawed hand. Meg leaned against Gertrude's tummy. They waited. Floyd came and joined them.

"What are you doing?" he asked.

"Waiting for Gertrude to come round," said Nellie. "She knocked herself out on the tree." Floyd screwed up his face. He thought waiting for a pretend dragon to come round boring.

"I'm going back to the swings," he said. "See you later." He tripped over Gertrude's tail and blinked when he saw nothing there.

A gust of wind blew the compress from Gertrude's ever-growing bump. Nellie carefully put it back. As she did so Gertrude groaned and opened first one eye, then the other.

"Where am I?" she said. She groaned again.

"You're in the park," said Nellie. "You hit the oak tree and knocked yourself out."

"My head hurts."

"You've got the biggest bump ever," said Nellie. Gertrude put up a hand to feel it.

"Careful," said Nellie.

"Ouch," said Gertrude. "I think I need to go to hospital."

"No, you don't," said Nellie. "But you're going to have a sore head for a few days."

"Oooh!" said Gertrude. "I am." A big tear rolled down her cheek. "I am," she sobbed.

Nellie put her arms around the dragon's neck and gave her a cuddle. "Don't worry, Gertrude. I'll take you home and tuck you up. I'll bathe your head and as a special treat, although you don't deserve it, you can have a packet of chocolate biscuits."

"Can I, Nellie? Can I really?"

Nellie nodded.

Shakily, Gertrude stood up. She felt a bit wobbly and the bump on her head throbbed. She looked across to where the park keeper was trying to sweep up flying leaves. With her hand on her head she staggered to the ever-blowing pile and with good aim and without breathing fire blew the whole lot into his wheelbarrow. As if it had all been too much trouble she raised the other hand to her head, leaving the surprised and pleased park keeper to trundle his barrow away before the wind blew the leaves out again.

"I shall never be so mean ever again," she said. "Never ever."

Nellie, Floyd and Meg caught Gertrude up at the gate. Gertrude felt too ill to fly home so Nellie held her hand and helped her along the pavement. Floyd couldn't work out what Nellie was doing.

At the front door Gertrude made a big effort and flew over the house to the garden.

"See you, Floyd," said Nellie.

"See you, Nellie," said Floyd.

Nellie and Meg went indoors. Nellie fetched the first aid things she needed and, with a quick look over her shoulder to make sure no one saw, took an unopened packet of chocolate biscuits from the cupboard. She put everything in a bag and carried it down the garden to the old shed.

Gertrude lay under her sacks, a hand on her head.

"How are you feeling?" said Nellie.

"My bump's throbbing like anything," said Gertrude. Nellie took out a plastic bag filled with ice cubes and a lump of cotton wool soaked in witch hazel.

"Put that on the bump," she said. Gertrude placed the cotton wool on the bump with the ice cubes on top and held them there.

"A dragon is likely to get arm ache," she said.

"It'll help the swelling to go down. You'll feel better by tomorrow. Anyway, you can take it off whenever you like."

"Did you bring me anything to eat?" said Gertrude. She eyed the bag hopefully. Nellie took out the chocolate biscuits. Gertrude smiled and winced as the skin pulled on the bump.

"Thank you, Nellie, kind friend," she said. "What would a dragon do without a kind friend like you?" Nellie laughed.

"I really don't know," she said. Nellie left Gertrude munching the chocolate biscuits.

"Let's hope she's learned a lesson," said Nellie, as she walked down the garden path. But, of course, you never know with dragons.

8 Nellie Buys a Kite

Nellie was finishing her breakfast when there was a knock at the front door. Meg ran to the door barking. Granny May was about to get up when Nellie said, "I'll go."

She chewed hard on her mouthful and swallowed. Her mouth was quite empty by the time she opened the door.

"Hello," she said. It was the postman.

"Morning," said the postman. "I hope he doesn't bite." He looked at Meg. Meg was wagging her tail and looking at him.

"Oh, no," said Nellie. "She doesn't." The postman handed Nellie a long, round parcel.

Then he got back in his van. Nellie closed the front door and carried the parcel into the kitchen. She wondered what it was. The address label said, "To Nellie Robinson."

"It's for me," said Nellie.

"Well, if it's for you," said Granny May, "you'd better open it." Granny May fetched a pair of scissors. "Be careful how you go," she said.

Nellie tugged at the sticky tape and snipped with the scissors. "I know," she cried. "I know what it is." There was a ripping sound as Nellie managed to get her finger under the brown paper. She pulled a piece off and it fell to the floor. Sam, Granny May's black-and-white cat, pounced. Splat! He landed on the paper. He pushed under it. He tossed the paper in the air and biffed it. When the next piece of paper fell he boxed with it and jumped and scrabbled.

Granny May laughed.

It took Nellie a long time to undo the parcel. It had been done up as though it was never meant to come undone again. At last she managed to unwrap all the brown paper. Next was a polythene bag. Through it Nellie could see red-and-yellow fabric.

"It is," she cried. "At last. It's my kite!"

Four weeks ago Nellie had sent off for a build-it-yourself red-and-yellow box kite from a kite and balloon factory. Four weeks was a long time ago. When it hadn't come within the first week Nellie had forgotten all about it. But here it was. Nellie cut the end from the polythene bag.

"Hold on," said Granny May. "Let me clear the table before you take all the bits out. You don't want to lose any."

"Good idea," said Nellie.

As Granny May put the dirty breakfast things by the sink, Nellie picked up all the bits of brown paper. They were scattered all over the floor. Sam had given up playing with them. He was curled up next to Meg in Meg's basket, just looking. Soon, Nellie knew, he would be fast asleep.

When the table was clear, Nellie wiped up the crumbs with a damp cloth. Granny May ran the tea towel over it to make sure it was nice and dry. Nellie tipped the contents of the polythene bag onto the table. The bits and pieces clattered and bounced.

"There should be instructions amongst that lot," said Granny May.

"Here they are," said Nellie. She unfolded a piece of paper that was covered with diagrams and writing.

"Mmm," said Granny May. "It looks quite complicated. Would you like me to help?"

"Yes, please," said Nellie.

Granny May fetched her spectacles and began reading the instructions. Nellie began to sort out the bits and pieces. There was the red-and-yellow fabric cover for the kite, a big ball of string wound round a wooden handle, big sticks and little sticks.

"It's not so difficult, it seems," said Granny

May. "Have a look." Nellie looked. "You have to fit the sticks into the corners of the kite. They've made the corners extra strong, it says."

"Shall we have a go?" said Nellie.

"I think we should," said Granny May.

Fitting the first sticks was easy. It got more difficult as they went on. The kite began to look like a box when they started on the fourth corner. It was quite tricky. They had a struggle getting the end of the last stick in, but they managed it at last.

"Phew," said Nellie.

"Goodness," said Granny May. "That was a tough one." They looked at the red-and-yellow kite as it sat on the table.

"It's big," said Nellie.

"It's magnificent," said Granny May.

"The only thing we need now is wind," said Nellie. She went into the garden and stood on the lawn. A slight breeze rustled the leaves on the old apple tree. Disappointed, she went indoors.

"There's no wind," she said.

"That's the trouble with flying kites," said Granny May. "You need the right weather. We'll have to keep listening to the weather forecast."

Nellie put the kite on the sideboard and went outside again. She sat on the garden wall, drumming her heels on the bricks and staring at the sky. She was wondering how long it would be before there was enough wind to blow the kite into the air.

"Yoo hoo! Nellie! Look at me!"

Nellie turned and looked down the garden. She saw Gertrude on the wall, balancing on her tail and wriggling her feet in the air. Nellie grinned.

"You want to be careful doing that on the wall, you might fall off."

"A dragon never falls off," said Gertrude. She had no sooner said it than her tail gave a wobble and she was tumbling over.

"Ouch," she said as she landed in the flowerbed.

"You all right?" Nellie asked, jumping off the wall to see.

"A dragon is always all right," said Gertrude. She brushed herself down.

"The pansies aren't," said Nellie. She looked at the squashed flowers.

"One of life's little accidents," said Gertrude. She tried to unsquash them but the pansies wouldn't stand up.

"Let's hope that's what Dad thinks when he sees them," said Nellie.

"You a bit glum?" asked Gertrude.

"Not really. Only I was hoping for a bit more wind," said Nellie.

"Oh, yes?" said Gertrude.

Nellie told Gertrude about the kite she and Granny May had put together. Gertrude listened carefully.

"Red and yellow. How nice," said Gertrude.

"And it's a box kite."

"A box kite. Yes, yes, I know," nodded Gertrude.

"The thing is, there's no wind and I really wanted to fly it today."

"You don't need wind," cried Gertrude. "You need me. I'll fly it for you."

"Will you, will you really?" said Nellie.

"For you, Nellie, I'll fly anything." Nellie was very pleased.

95

"Meet me in the park at the top of the hill in fifteen minutes. I'm off to limber up," said Gertrude. Nellie raced indoors. She grabbed the kite and the string.

"Where are you off to?" said Granny May.

"To fly the kite in the park," said Nellie. "I'm going to see if Floyd wants to come." Granny May looked doubtful.

"There's not enough wind," she said.

"I know," said Nellie. Granny May was about to say something else but Nellie had gone.

Yes, Floyd did want to come too. He and Nellie raced along the pavement to the stares of passers-by. It wasn't until they went through the park gates that Floyd suddenly stopped. He licked a finger and lifted it in the air.

"Nellie," he said, "there's no wind."

"We don't need wind. Gertrude's going to fly it for me."

"Oh yeah," said Floyd.

"Honestly," said Nellie. A disbelieving look spread over Floyd's face.

"Come on," said Nellie. "You'll see."

Nellie ran on. She could see Gertrude at the top of the hill doing arm swings and knee bends. Floyd followed reluctantly. It seemed a bit suspicious to him. A kite can't be flown without wind. That was obvious. As for an invisible dragon flying it instead, that was too much to

96

believe.

Nellie arrived at the top of the hill quite out of breath.

"You're a bit puffed, aren't you?" said Gertrude. She was doing stretching-on-one-leg exercises.

"I ran all the way here," said Nellie.

"Not enough keep-fit if you ask me," said Gertrude, changing legs. Nellie waited for her to finish her stretch.

"You should try this, Nellie. It's very good for muscle tone," said Gertrude.

Nellie didn't want to try it, she wanted to get on with flying her kite. She didn't say anything. Experience had taught her that with Gertrude you had to wait until Gertrude was ready. Gertrude did one final stretch.

"Right," she said. "This dragon is fit and ready for take-off. Hand me the kite." Nellie handed Gertrude the kite.

"Unwind the string." Nellie unwound the string.

"Are you ready?" Nellie nodded. She was ready.

"Then off we go."

Gertrude raised her large wings and, spreading them wide, took off. The kite rose into the air. Nellie let out the string as fast as she could. Up and up went Gertrude. Up and up went the kite until it seemed almost a speck in the sky.

Floyd was still at the bottom of the hill. He hadn't wanted to go up. He had been overcome with an uncomfortable feeling that Nellie was trying to make a fool of him. He could hardly believe his eyes when he saw Nellie holding the string handle and the kite miles above, bobbing and weaving as though it was a really windy day.

Gertrude was having a lovely time. The bobbing and weaving was caused by her letting go of the kite and diving to catch it as it plummeted earthwards. She looped the loop and turned somersaults with it. She did backward flips and forward rolls. It was great fun.

Nellie was enjoying herself at her end of the string too. Several times she had almost been lifted from the ground. She had hung on. It was like flying the kite in a gale. When Gertrude let go she ran backwards and when Gertrude took hold again she ran forwards. It was very exciting.

When Floyd got to the top of the hill, Nellie said, "Want a go?"

Floyd wasn't sure. He couldn't see why the kite was in the air. It was odd looking at a kite high in the air on a windless day.

"Here," said Nellie thrusting the string handle at him. "It's great."

In spite of himself. Floyd found that it was fun. He couldn't make out why the string went slack but when Nellie said, "Run backwards," he did. As for running forwards, he didn't have much choice about that. The kite pulled him.

Everything went really well until Gertrude made a mistake. She did a particularly complicated forward roll across the kite and her feet became caught up in the string. By the time she stopped rolling, her hands and feet were quite tied up and the kite was caught above her head. Luckily her wings were still free.

"Help," she said. "I'd better land and let Nellie undo me. I'm in a proper pickle." She looked down and saw Nellie waving and pointing to the great beech tree below her.

Nellie couldn't make out what had happened to Gertrude. All she knew was something terrible had happened to Floyd. There had been an almighty tug on the string. Instead of letting go, Floyd had hung on and been carried high into the air. He had swept across the sky until he became tangled in the beech tree. He'd let go of the string and clung onto a branch. There he was, petrified with fright, stuck at the top of a tree which was too big to climb down.

It didn't take the park keeper long to arrive,

his face twitching with fury.

"What's that boy doing in my beech tree?" he demanded.

"He's stuck," said Nellie.

"Stuck!" The park keeper's eyes nearly popped out of his head. "Stuck! I suppose I've got to phone for the fire brigade to come and get him down. I don't know why they let children in the park. More trouble than they're worth, they are. I've got enough to do without this." He stomped off down the hill muttering all the way.

Gertrude came in to land. As she touched down, the kite landed over her head. She was a tied-up tangle of string.

"I'm quite done up," she chuckled. "Can you take the kite off my head, Nellie?" Nellie pulled the kite from Gertrude's head.

"What's the matter?" said Gertrude, seeing

Nellie's alarmed face.

"It's Floyd. He's stuck in the beech tree."

"How did he get there?" said Gertrude.

"He was holding the kite. You pulled him there."

"Well, there's not much I can do about it until you untie me," said Gertrude. Nellie looked at the tangle Gertrude was in. She wrung her hands.

"I haven't got time. Old grumpy's phoning for the fire brigade. When they come Floyd'll get in terrible trouble."

"Why?" said Gertrude. "They'll get him down."

"Yes," said Nellie. "But they'll think he climbed up and no one's supposed to climb the trees in the park. They'll never believe how he really got there."

"Well," said Gertrude with a sigh. "We'll have to break the string."

"I don't mind honestly," said Nellie.

Gertrude took a deep breath. There was a roaring sound. Slowly she breathed out, singeing the string with her hot breath until it snapped. Nellie pulled at the ends and soon Gertrude was free.

"Get on my back, Nellie," said Gertrude.

Nellie climbed up. She put her arms around Gertrude's neck and hung on as Gertrude spread her wings. When they reached Floyd, he was clinging to the tree like a limpet. Gertrude perched by him on the branch.

"Shut your eyes," said Nellie.

"I can't let go," he said.

"Yes, you can," said Nellie. "Shut your eyes and hold on to me."

Floyd shut his eyes. It made letting go of the tree easier but he couldn't see how holding onto Nellie would get him down. With eyes tightly shut he stretched out an arm. Gertrude took it and lifted him up. Holding him tightly in her arms she flew into the air. She landed near the bottom of the tree. She sat Floyd on the ground. Nellie slid from Gertrude's back and sat beside him.

"You can open your eyes now," said Nellie. Floyd opened his eyes and blinked. He touched the ground.

"How did I get down?" he asked.

"Gertrude flew you down," said Nellie.

"But . . . I can't see her," he said.

"Perhaps," said Nellie, "perhaps one day you will. Come on. Let's get out of here before the fire brigade arrives and we get into trouble." Nellie pulled Floyd to his feet. She picked up the kite and string handle. There wasn't time to pick up the bits of string. She and Floyd ran all the way to the park gates.

As they reached the pavement they heard the fire engine coming down the street, its siren blaring. Nellie grinned.

"Old grumpy's going to have a lot of explaining to do," she said.

"Yeah," said Floyd weakly. "He is." He could hardly believe he had been stuck at the top of the beech tree. But he must have been, otherwise why would old grumpy have telephoned the fire brigade? Floyd shook his head.

"Crumbs," he said as the two of them turned for home. "Perhaps there really *is* a dragon, after all."

9 Nellie and the Runaway Skateboard

Nellie was upstairs in her room going through her toy cupboard. Granny May said it needed a good clear out. Nellie hadn't wanted to do it but once she started she could see Granny May had been right. She was enjoying herself too. Granny May's head came round the door.

"How are you getting on?" she asked.

"Really well," said Nellie. "I don't need any of these any more." She pointed to a large pile of things in the middle of the carpet. There were all kinds of bits and pieces there, including lots and lots of old comics.

"Oh, well done," said Granny May. "You

have been busy." Nellie rummaged at the back of the cupboard.

"What's this?" she said, pulling out a red board with wheels on. "Oh, my skateboard. I'd forgotten all about it."

"So had I," said Granny May.

"Oh, I'm glad I found that. Can I take it to the park and have a go on it today?" asked Nellie.

"You can," said Granny May. "But finish your tidying first."

Nellie threw herself into finishing the tidying. She was so excited to have found the skateboard. Finding it was like receiving a present. Granny May came upstairs with the vacuum cleaner and Nellie helped her suck up all the dust and tiny bits of debris left in the cupboard. Nellie put everything she was keeping neatly back on the shelves. It looked very tidy when it was finished.

"Well done," said Granny May. "You deserve a trip to the park after that. Are you going to ask Floyd to go with you?"

"Can I?" said Nellie.

"Of course you can," said Granny May. "I'll have a special tea ready for you when you come back."

Nellie pulled on her sweatshirt, grabbed Meg's lead and ball, tucked the skateboard under her arm and, with Meg pulling hard, set off. She banged on Floyd's front door. Floyd's eyes lit up when he saw the skateboard.

"I'd forgotten you'd got that," he said.

"So had I," said Nellie. "You coming to the park?"

"You bet." Floyd ran to tell his mum he was going out with Nellie.

"And ask if you can come to tea," Nellie called after him. He was back in a jiffy.

"I can," he said pleased.

They walked quickly to the park, Floyd held the lead and Nellie carried the skateboard. As soon as they were through the park gates, Floyd unclipped the lead and Nellie put the skateboard on the path. Meg ran off to dig. Nellie pushed herself along on the skateboard.

"Let's go to the hill," said Nellie.

"Good idea," said Floyd. He ran along beside her.

Nellie let Floyd have first go down the hill. He sat on the skateboard as if it was a toboggan. It rolled down for a long way. Floyd waved when he got off and scootered back up the hill. When it got steep he picked up the skateboard and carried it.

"Your turn," he said when he got to the top. He was puffed. He sat and watched as Nellie stood on the skateboard and, with arms outstretched, launched herself down the hill.

She went really well and was slowing down towards the bottom when the park keeper, who wasn't looking, pushed a wheelbarrow across her path. The skateboard went one way and Nellie the other. She landed in the wheelbarrow on top of a pile of weeds.

"What do you think you're up to?" said the park keeper.

"Nothing," said Nellie. She climbed out of the wheelbarrow.

"I suppose you're going to say that was my fault," said the park keeper. "Let me tell you I work hard, day in day out, to keep this park tidy."

Nellie wondered what that had to do with anything. She brushed herself down. Floyd came running up.

"You all right," he asked.

"Yup, fine," said Nellie.

"Just you keep out of my way and I'll keep out of yours," said the park keeper. He wheeled his wheelbarrow down the path without a backward glance.

"That's just what he didn't do," said Floyd. Nellie shrugged and picked up the skateboard.

"Want another go?" she asked Floyd.

"Yeah," he said. "Do you?" Nellie nodded.

"Let's hope old grumpy doesn't come back with his wheelbarrow. We might not be so lucky next time," she said.

When they reached the top of the hill Floyd positioned his foot on the skateboard.

"You going down standing?" asked Nellie.

"Yup," said Floyd and he was off. As the skateboard gathered speed he lifted his other foot onto the board. Balancing carefully he steered himself down the hill.

"Well done," yelled Nellie after him. "That's great, Floyd."

Somewhere near the bottom of the slope, as he was slowing down, Floyd hit a bump. He went one way and the skateboard the other. Only instead of slowing down and stopping, the skateboard gathered speed and whizzed along the path towards the lake.

"Nellie," yelled Floyd. "The skateboard's gone!"

Nellie knew. She had watched the whole thing from the top of the hill and was cross.

"It's the dragon," she called. "As soon as she saw you fall off she swooped down and stole it. Come on, we've got to try and get it back."

"The dragon!" said Floyd. "How could a dragon steal a skateboard?"

"She just did," said Nellie. "Let's go before she wrecks it."

Gertrude had never been on a skateboard before. She had watched how Floyd had stood on one leg and pushed himself along with the other. That was all right. It was when she wanted to put both feet on the board that she had a problem. Her feet were large. One foot would fit, two feet wouldn't. Gertrude solved the problem by putting one foot on top of the other. This made balancing more difficult and steering rather dangerous. She managed somehow and the further she went the better she got at it.

Gertrude pushed herself along the path by the lake, loving every minute of it. Meg saw Gertrude coming and ran towards her, growling and chewing her ball. She wanted Gertrude to play. Gertrude had other ideas.

"Go away, Meg, or I'll run you over," cried Gertrude. "Beware all dogs that get in my way."

Meg, taking no heed of this warning, dropped her ball and ran alongside the skateboard, barking and nipping at Gertrude's ankles.

"Go away, Meg," said Gertrude. "Go away."

Gertrude was so busy trying to wallop Meg and stay on the skateboard at the same time that she forgot to look where she was going. Meg stopped in time, Gertrude didn't. The skateboard did a neat dive over a bank, dropping itself and Gertrude into the lake. There was a little splash and a big splash. Meg, realizing that this accident may have had something to do with her, ran off to find her ball.

Gertrude was furious. The ducks paddled over to have a look. Gertrude was standing in the water with bits of weed hanging from her ears. The skateboard was too heavy to float. Gertrude had to feel her way across the muddy lake bed for it.

"Ah, got it," she said at last and lifted it out of the water. Gertrude clambered back up the bank. She picked the weed from the skateboard and was about to pick it from herself when she noticed Nellie and Floyd running towards her.

"Tee hee, can't catch me," she said and skated off, the weed round her ears blowing behind her.

"Oh, no," said Nellie. "We'll never catch her now."

Gertrude skated round the path to the park gate. Steering was still not Gertrude's strong point and she had a narrow miss with a woman and a pram. The woman stared, alarmed by the fast-moving skateboard without a rider. She didn't see the dragon pushing it along, her tail waving from side to side as she went.

"This is going to be fun," said Gertrude, reaching the park gate. Not stopping and hardly looking, she skated into the road. An oncoming car braked hard to avoid the skateboard. The car behind it braked too but not quickly enough. There was a horrible crunch as it ran into the back of the car in front. Both cars stopped and the drivers got out. Gertrude didn't stop. Skating on the road was much smoother than on the bumpy path in the park.

"Tee hee, can't catch me," said Gertrude. She pushed herself along, gathering speed and dodging in and out of the traffic. Cars were stopping and hooting and steering this way and that to avoid the runaway skateboard. Behind her Gertrude left a trail of chaos but she didn't care.

She whizzed by a notice on the road which said "Caution. Traffic Lights Out Of Order" but she didn't bother to read it. At the traffic lights a policeman in a glowing orange jacket was directing the traffic. The traffic going Gertrude's way was waiting. Gertrude didn't wait. She zoomed down the outside of the queue, reached the policeman and did an elegant turn around him. The policeman, not seeing the dragon, stared open-mouthed at the skateboard. Not being able to follow it, as he was directing the traffic, he reached for his radio and said,

"Runaway skateboard in Hanley Street proceeding in direction of park." He went back to directing the traffic but kept looking over his shoulder at the skateboard nipping in and out between the cars.

As Gertrude made her way back to the park, the sound of an approaching police-car siren followed her. She looked over her shoulder and saw a flashing blue light. Gertrude pushed herself along even faster. It occurred to her that the flashing blue light and siren might just have something to do with her. After all, she had just broken all the rules in the Highway Code and whizzing round a policeman had been rather a silly thing to do.

"I must have been reported," she cried. "Tee hee, can't catch me." Gertrude whizzed across the oncoming traffic into the park. Cars squealed to a halt. The police car followed her. Nellie and Floyd jumped off the path onto the grass to make way for the skateboard and the police car following it.

"Oh, no," said Nellie. "This time they really will arrest her. It'll be for dangerous driving."

"Nellie, do you think the police'll catch it?" said Floyd. "Come on, let's see what happens."

What happened was one of those unexpected things. The unsuspecting park keeper, not looking for the second time that day, pushed his wheelbarrow across the path. This happened as Gertrude was looking over her shoulder to see how near the police car was. She hit the wheelbarrow with a bang. This time it was the skateboard which ended up amongst the weeds. Gertrude took a dive over the barrow into a holly bush hedge. It was lucky for her that dragons are scaly-skinned. She didn't feel too many prickles but she did feel sorry for herself.

Two burly policemen jumped from the police car. They dived on the skateboard and lifted it from the wheelbarrow as if it were something alive that could escape at any minute. It was only on closer inspection that they realized the skateboard was incapable of going anywhere without a rider.

"That blooming skateboard. That's the second time it's hit me today," said the park keeper. "I can't spend all day avoiding skateboards. I've too much to do." With that he trundled the wheelbarrow off to the compost heap, leaving the policemen standing there.

"What are we going to do with it?" said one of the policemen.

"It must belong to somebody," said the other.

"It's mine," said Nellie.

"Oh, is it?" said the first policeman. "This skateboard's been causing an awful lot of trouble."

"I'm very sorry. I won't let it happen again," said Nellie.

"No, don't," said the policeman. He handed Nellie the skateboard. "Better take it home." With that the two policemen got back in the car and drove backwards out of the park.

Nellie turned to Gertrude, who was still in the holly hedge. "I suppose you want a hand out?"

"Yes, please," said Gertrude meekly. Nellie pulled and Gertrude came out of the hedge with much scratching of prickles on dragon scales.

"I think I'll go home and have a little lie down. I feel a little prickled."

"Good idea," said Nellie.

At home, when Nellie and Floyd were having their tea, Floyd said, "If it wasn't a dragon, how did the skateboard move?"

"Exactly," said Nellie and took another bite of cake.

"Mmm," said Floyd. "Something made it move. I suppose it *could* have been a dragon."

10 Nellie Goes to the Seaside

Floyd rang Nellie's front door bell. He was ready to go. He carried a large ball, his swimming things and some cheese straws his mum had made specially. Meg barked on the other side of the door.

"Good morning, Floyd," said Mr Patel. He was on the way to his shop. "And where are you off to on this fine morning?"

"I'm going to the seaside with Nellie and Nellie's dad and gran."

"A perfect day for it. Have a lovely time," said Mr Patel.

"Thanks, Mr Patel," said Floyd.

"Going to the seaside," a voice echoed from the top of the lamp-post. Floyd looked round. He thought someone had said something but there was no one there. Nellie opened the front door.

"We're nearly ready," said Nellie. "Dad says to put your things in the car. I've got the key."

As Nellie unlocked the boot there was a thud on the car roof. A face lowered itself to Nellie's and said,

"I want to come to the seaside too!"

"All right," said Nellie looking up. "Only no funny business."

"Certainly not," said the face which belonged, of course, to Gertrude the dragon.

Floyd looked to where Nellie was looking. There was nothing there. He shrugged. It seemed as if Nellie was talking to herself. He knew she would say she was talking to the dragon. But what dragon? On the other hand so many funny things had happened recently. Floyd looked really hard. Something glinted in the sunlight. He blinked.

"Sunlight on the roof," he said to himself. Gertrude looked at Floyd looking at her.

"If he made a bit more effort he could see me," she said.

"Floyd could?"

"Yes, if he tried harder," said Gertrude. "He's

117

beginning to think there might be something in dragons, I can tell." With that Gertrude flew onto the lamp-post. Floyd blinked again.

"Did you see her?" Nellie asked.

"No." Floyd shook his head. "No. But something glinted."

"The sun on her scales," said Nellie.

"Do you think so?" said Floyd. "I'm not sure."

Dad and Granny May struggled through the front door with a pile of things. Dad had a picnic basket and two fold-up chairs. Granny May was carrying three bags and had Meg on the lead pulling hard to get to the car.

"Take the dog, Nellie, before I drop everything," said Granny May.

"Let me take a bag," said Floyd.

"Thank you, Floyd," said Granny May. "We've got rather a lot of stuff as usual."

Nellie took Meg and opened the car door so she could jump in. She was very excited, and her pink tongue lolled out as she panted. Meg loved going in the car. Nellie helped Floyd put the bag in the boot along with the picnic basket, chairs and other bags. It was a squash. At last everyone tumbled into the car. Granny May was driving there and Dad was driving back.

"That's fair," Granny May had said. She started the engine and they were off.

"Wait for me," cried Gertrude from the lamp-post. Nellie heard a thud on the roof. She looked out of the back window at Gertrude's tail waving in the breeze. Gertrude will enjoy the seaside, Nellie thought.

It didn't take too long to drive out of town. Dad got out the map to make sure they were going the right way. Granny May said he needn't bother.

"I know the way like the back of my hand," she said.

It was a long drive before Nellie saw the sea glinting between the hills in the distance. From that moment she wished they could be there now. After what seemed like ages they were following a sign which said "To The Car Park."

"At last," said Nellie, when Granny May switched off the engine. She jumped out and Meg scrambled after her.

"Come on, Floyd," she said. "I'll race you to the beach."

Nellie, Meg and Floyd tore down the path to the beach. Someone had already beaten them to it. It was Gertrude. She was lying in the warm sand, wriggling her body and stretching her neck. "It's lovely," she called to Nellie. "Just what a dragon likes. A sand bath. Oooh! It's lovely." Nellie left Gertrude to her sand bath and raced after Floyd and Meg who were at the water's edge.

"Do you think it's cold?" said Nellie.

"Only one way to find out," said Floyd. He took off his shoes and socks. The next wave broke over his feet.

"Well?" said Nellie.

"It's freezing."

"Let me try," said Nellie. She pulled off her trainers and socks and went into the water. "It is a bit cold," she said. "But we'll soon get used to it."

Meg wasn't at all sure about the waves. As they curled over and broke she barked and as they flowed up the beach she backed off.

"What was Nellie doing in the water?" Meg wondered and barked some more.

Paddling was fun once they'd got used to the chill of the sea. They wriggled their toes and squeezed sand between them. Even Meg got her feet wet in the end.

"Let's go and get our swimming things on," said Nellie.

"Good idea," said Floyd. "I'd like a swim."

As they turned back up the beach, Gertrude came crowing towards them, scuffing up sand with her large feet.

"I've had my sand bath. I'm going swimming," she said. "A dragon needs to swim. It's good for the keep-fit. Oh, indeed, yes." With that she ran past them. Nellie watched as she waded into the sea and plunged in. Gertrude didn't swim on top of the water, she swam under it and Nellie watched anxiously until she came up for air. Gertrude waved. Nellie waved back. She turned and followed Floyd.

Dad was coming swimming with them. He and Granny May had put up the chairs and laid out the rugs. They had put up a windbreak to shelter the chosen spot from the breeze.

"We'll be very comfortable here," Granny May said and settled in a chair with her newspaper.

They changed quickly and raced down the

beach to the water.

"It's cold, Dad," Nellie warned as Dad ran in.

"No it's not," said Dad. "It's lovely and warm."

Nellie and Floyd were surprised to find that Dad was right.

"Warmed it up for you," cried Gertrude from further out. "The least a dragon can do for her friends."

"Thanks, Gertrude," said Nellie. Gertrude took a deep breath and disappeared beneath the surface. Nellie saw a trail of bubbles popping on the water where Gertrude was blowing out hot air. No wonder the water was warmer.

"I just hope it doesn't get too hot," said Nellie.

"Come on in, Nellie," said Floyd. "It's great".

Nellie waded into the water until it was deep enough for her to swim. The water was lovely. Nellie hoped it wasn't too hot for any nearby fish. Dad was enjoying a relaxing float on his back. Floyd and Nellie decided to have a race.

"On your marks, get set, go!" cried Nellie. They swam their fastest. Suddenly Nellie felt something underneath her. Gertrude's head came to the surface in front of her face.

"Hold on to my neck," said Gertrude. "I'll give you a ride."

It was either that or fall into the water so

Nellie held on. Gertrude swam with an elegant breast stroke. Floyd was soon left behind. When he stopped swimming at what he thought was the winning post, there was no sign of Nellie.

Floyd was astonished. He put his feet on the bottom and stood up. Nellie was a long way away and right out of her depth.

"Come back," called Floyd. "It's not safe to be so far out."

"It's all right," Nellie called back. "I'm on Gertrude. She's giving me a ride. It's wonderful."

At the sound of the raised voices Dad stopped floating and looked up. He saw Floyd but he couldn't see Nellie.

"Where's Nellie?" he asked alarmed.

"Out there," said Floyd pointing. Nellie was so far out that she was a tiny speck bobbing between the waves.

"What does she think she's doing?" said Dad.

"Going for a ride on the dragon," said Floyd. Dad was furious.

"Nellie, come back here at once," he shouted. "At once."

"Better take me back, Gertrude," said Nellie. "I can see Dad waving."

"Rotten old spoilsport," said Gertrude. "Just when we were having fun. I'll show him."

Gertrude got up speed until her body came out of the water. Spreading her wings she launched herself into the air. Nellie held on tightly. They skimmed across the waves, the tips of Gertrude's wings blowing up spray with each powerful movement. Before she got to Dad she put out her legs and braked sharply, throwing up a massive spray which cascaded over him. She gave a wriggle. Nellie fell off and splashed into the water by Dad.

"Serves him right for spoiling a dragon's fun and a dragon's friend's fun." With that Gertrude plunged under the next wave, leaving a trail of hot bubbles.

Spluttering, Dad took hold of Nellie as if he couldn't believe it was her.

"How did you get back so quickly?" he asked. "I don't believe it's you." Nellie spat out a mouthful of salty water.

"It's me all right," she said.

Floyd had watched everything carefully. He knew that Nellie couldn't have swum that fast by herself. How had she done it? He hadn't exactly seen anything, except something glinting.

"The sun on the water?" he wondered. He shook his head. "No, it was something else."

As the three of them came out of the water, Meg ran down the beach to greet them. Granny May handed out towels and told them not to drip on the rugs. While they dried themselves she unpacked the picnic.

"Don't forget the cheese straws," said Floyd.

"I won't," said Granny May.

The picnic was a great success. Even Meg had a special bone biscuit. It was Gertrude who felt left out. She leaned her head over the windbreak and, dripping onto Nellie's T-shirt, whispered, "Where's mine? A dragon needs a little something to keep her going, you know."

Nellie hadn't fogotten her. She handed Gertrude a large paper bag. No one seemed to notice. Granny May and Dad were dozing and Floyd was playing with Meg.

"This is for you," she said. "It's a selection. I

saved it."

"Thank you, Nellie. Thank you," said Gertrude. She was so delighted she gave Nellie a dragon kiss. It was rather a wet one and meant Nellie had to wipe her face with her sleeve. Gertrude opened the bag and, muddling everything up, munched cheese straws with chocolate cake and egg sandwiches with an orange. She enjoyed every mouthful.

"Delicious. Delicious," she spluttered.

Gertrude handed Nellie the empty bag and decided to have forty winks. She stretched out on the sand and closed her eyes. She opened them again when a shower of sand sprayed across her face. Meg was digging with her ball. Gertrude picked up the ball and threw it. Meg raced after it. Gertrude closed her eyes and began another doze. She was awakened by another shower of sand.

"That does it!" she said. She picked up the ball and threw it into the air, took a deep breath and was about to blast the ball when she sneezed. Her head jerked downwards. The hot blast missed the ball and fell on the sand next to Dad's shoes. The heat was so great the sand melted and before Gertrude could stop them the shoes fell into the molten puddle.

"Oh, dear, whoops a daisy," she said. Meg grabbed the ball and ran.

As the molten puddle cooled, Gertrude could see she had made glass.

"Most interesting," she said. She picked up the shoes which were inside a glass blob. "I did that all by myself. I think it's rather nice."

Dad was puzzled when he saw the shoes. He couldn't decide how such a thing had happened. The nice thing was that he was in such a good mood that he didn't seem to mind. He said he was going to keep the shoes in the blob and put them on the mantelpiece. Granny May frowned.

"Not if I can help it," she said.

Dad had to drive them home in his socks and he didn't grumble once.

"Perhaps," Nellie thought, "just perhaps he's getting used to funny things happening."

Floyd was beginning to think that all the funny happenings meant there really *was* a dragon. He thought about it as they drove home. His biggest surprise was when he looked out of the back window. He was sure he could see a golden and green tail waving in the breeze.

"Wow!" he said and grinned.

SAMANTHA SLADE

Samantha Slade's an ordinary girl living in an ordinary town; but when she starts a job out of school babysitting for the Brown children, her uneventful life is turned upside down. Because when Dr Brown tells Samantha her children are little monsters, poor Sam doesn't realize that they really *are* monsters! Lupi turns into a werewolf when the moon is full, and Drake sprouts fangs, drinks tomato ketchup by the crateful and concocts the most amazing potions in his laboratory!

Book 1: **Monster-Sitter**

When Samantha Slade agrees to let Lupi and Drake Brown, the two children she babysits, help her with the school Halloween party, she finds she's created the most realistic haunted house ever! Lupi turns into a real werewolf, the fake creepie crawlies become alive, and the whole thing turns into a riot of terrified kids . . .

Book 2: **Confessions of a Teenage Frog**

Samantha Slade should have known better than to accept help from Lupi and Drake when she's campaigning to become class president. Drake makes her a "greatness potion", and before she knows it, she's been turned into a frog! Will Drake be able to turn her back again before she has to make her big speech for the campaign?

Other titles in the SAMANTHA SLADE series:
Book 3 **Our Friend, Public Nuisance No 1**
Book 4 **The Terrors of Rock and Roll**

HAUNTINGS by Hippo Books is a new series of excellent ghost stories for older readers.

Ghost Abbey by Robert Westall
When Maggie and her family move into a run-down old abbey, they begin to notice some very strange things going on in the rambling old building. Is there any truth in the rumour that the abbey is haunted?

Don't Go Near the Water by Carolyn Sloan
Brendan knew instinctively that he shouldn't go near Blackwater Lake. Especially that summer, when the water level was so low. But what was the dark secret that lurked in the depths of the lake?

Voices by Joan Aiken
Julia had been told by people in the village that Harkin House was haunted. And ever since moving in to the house for the summer, she'd been troubled by violent dreams. What had happened in the old house's turbulent past?

The Nightmare Man by Tessa Krailing
Alex first sees the man of his darkest dreams at Stackfield Pond. And soon afterwards he and his family move in to the old house near the pond — End House — and the nightmare man becomes more than just a dream.

A Wish at the Baby's Grave by Angela Bull
Desperate for some money, Cathy makes a wish for some at the baby's grave in the local cemetery. Straight afterwards, she finds a job at an old bakery. But there's something very strange about the bakery and the two Germans who work there. . .

The Bone-Dog by Susan Price
Susan can hardly believe her eyes when her uncle Bryan makes her a pet out of an old fox-fur, a bone and some drops of blood — and then brings it to life. It's wonderful to have a pet which follows her every command — until the bone-dog starts to obey even her unconscious thoughts. . .

All on a Winter's Day by Lisa Taylor
Lucy and Hugh wake up suddenly one wintry morning to find everything's changed — their mother's disappeared, the house is different, and there are two ghostly children and their evil-looking aunt in the house. What has happened?

The Old Man on a Horse by Robert Westall
Tobias couldn't understand what was happening. His parents and little sister had gone to Stonehenge with the hippies, and his father was arrested. Then his mother disappeared. But while sheltering with his sister in a barn, he finds a statue of an old man on a horse, and Tobias and Greta find themselves transported to the time of the Civil War. . .

Look out for these forthcoming titles in the HAUNTING series:
The Rain Ghost by Garry Kilworth
The Haunting of Sophy Bartholomew by Elizabeth Lindsay

THE MALL

Six teenagers, all from different backgrounds, with one
thing in common – they all want jobs at the new
shopping Mall opening in Monk's Way. But working at
the Mall brings rather more than most of them had
bargained for . . .

Book 1: **Setting Up Shop**

Book 2: **Open for Business**
The new shopping Mall is opening soon, and the six
teenagers who work there are already having problems. Ian
is fired from his job at Harmony Records because of his
dad's interference. Amanda's trying to fend of Mr Grozzi's
advances at the restaurant. Jake's trying to hold down two
jobs at once. And Simon's temper is threatening to cost
him his job at the furniture store. Will life at the Mall prove
too tough to handle?.

Look out for the next books in The Mall series:

Book 3: **Gangs, Ghosts and Gypsies**
Book 4: **Money Matters**

You'll find these and many more fun Hippo books at
your local bookseller, or you can order them direct. Just
send off to *Customer Services, Hippo Books, Westfield
Road, Southam, Leamington Spa, Warwickshire CV33
0JH*, not forgetting to enclose a cheque or postal order
for the price of the book(s) plus 30p for postage and
packing.

MORGAN SWIFT

Morgan Swift is twenty-four, stunningly beautiful,
independent, a great runner, and a fabulous science
teacher. And she has the knack of finding trouble – and
getting out of it!

MORGAN SWIFT AND THE MINDMASTER

Morgan Swift has an extraordinary ability – she has the
power of second sight. And when her mental powers
warn her that some of her pupils at Coolidge High are in
trouble, she decides to investigate. It's not long before
she finds the culprit – a cult leader called Yang who's
been giving the kids extra coaching after school . . .

MORGAN SWIFT AND THE TRAIL OF THE JAGUAR

Morgan Swift's two pupils, Jenny Wu and Sally
Jackson, are thrilled to be going on holiday with their
favourite teacher. And they can't believe their luck when
an old friend of Morgan's, the attractive Tom Saunders,
invites them to go on an ultra-secret archaeological dig
in the South American jungle. But when things start to
go wrong, they turn to their teacher to find out exactly
what's going on in the jungle . . .

Watch out for more titles in the thrilling
MORGAN SWIFT series:

MORGAN SWIFT AND THE LAKE OF DIAMONDS
MORGAN SWIFT AND THE RIDDLE OF THE SPHINX

HIPPO ACTIVITY BOOKS

Feeling bored? Get into some of these activity books on
the Hippo list – from Postman Pat to Defenders of the
Earth, there is plenty of fun to be had by all!

THE DISNEY QUIZ AND PUZZLE BOOK II	The Walt Disney Company	£1.25
MILES OF FUN	Penny Kitchenham	£1.95
ADVENTURE IN SPACE	Janet McKellar and Jenny Bullough	£1.95
THE HAUNTED CASTLE		£1.95
COUNTRYSIDE ACTIVITY BOOK		£1.95
THE DINOSAUR FUN BOOK	Gillian Osband	£1.95
THE ANTI-COLOURING BOOK	Susan Striker	£2.75
THE MAGIC MIRROR BOOK	Marion Walter	£1.75
THE SECOND MAGIC MIRROR BOOK	Marion Walter	£1.50
THE SUMMER ACTIVITY BOOK	Hannah Glease	£2.25
THE HOLIDAY FUN BOOK		£1.95
POSTMAN PAT'S SONGBOOK	Bryan Daly	£1.75
THE SPRING BOOK	Troy Alexander	£2.25
THE DEEP FREEZE ADVENTURE COLOURING BOOK		£0.75

You'll find these and many more fun Hippo books at
your local bookseller, or you can order them direct. Just
send off to *Customer Services, Hippo Books, Westfield
Road, Southam, Leamington Spa, Warwickshire CV33
0JH*, not forgetting to enclose a cheque or postal order
for the price of the book(s) plus 30p per book for postage
and packing.

HIPPO BESTSELLERS

If you enjoyed this book, why not look out for other bestselling Hippo titles. You'll find gripping novels, fun activity books, fascinating non-fiction, crazy humour and sensational poetry books for all ages and tastes.

THE GHOSTBUSTERS STORYBOOK	Anne Digby	£2.50
SNOOKERED	Michael Hardcastle	£1.50
BENJI THE HUNTED	Walt Disney Company	£2.25
NELLIE AND THE DRAGON	Elizabeth Lindsay	£1.75
ALIENS IN THE FAMILY	Margaret Mahy	£1.50
HARRIET AND THE CROCODILES	Martin Waddell	£1.25
MAKE ME A STAR 1: PRIME TIME	Susan Beth Pfeffer	£1.50
THE SPRING BOOK	Troy Alexander	£2.25
SLEUTH!	Sherlock Ransford	£1.50
THE SPOOKTACULAR JOKE BOOK	Theodore Freek	£1.25
ROLAND RAT'S RODENT JOKE BOOK		£1.25
THE LITTLE VAMPIRE	Angela Sommer-Bodenberg	£1.25
POSTMAN PAT AND THE GREENDALE GHOST	John Cunliffe	£1.50
POSTMAN PAT AND THE CHRISTMAS PUDDING	John Cunliffe	£1.50

You'll find these and many more fun Hippo books at your local bookseller, or you can order them direct. Just send off to *Customer Services, Hippo Books, Westfield Road, Southam, Leamington Spa, Warwickshire CV33 OJH*, not forgetting to enclose a cheque or postal order for the price of the book(s) plus 30p per book for postage and packing.

HIPPO BOOKS FOR OLDER READERS

If you enjoy a good read, look out for all the Hippo books that are available for older readers. You'll find gripping adventure stories, romance novels, spooky ghost stories and all sorts of fun fiction.

CHEERLEADERS NO 2: GETTING EVEN	Christopher Pike	£1.25
CHEERLEADERS NO 3: RUMOURS	Caroline B Cooney	£1.25
ANIMAL INN 1: PETS ARE FOR KEEPS	Virginia Vail	£1.50
MEGASTAR	Jean Ure	£1.50
SOMERSAULTS	Michael Hardcastle	£1.50
THE LITTLE GYMNAST	Sheila Haigh	£1.25
CREEPS	Tim Schoch	£1.50
THE GREAT FLOOD MYSTERY	Jane Curry	£1.75
GET LAVINIA GOODBODY!	Roger Collinson	£1.25
AM I GOING WITH YOU?	Thurley Fowler	£1.25
THE KARATE KID: PART II	B B Hiller	£1.25
KEVIN AND THE IRON POODLE	J K Hooper	£1.25

You'll find these and many more fun Hippo books at your local bookseller, or you can order them direct. Just send off to *Customer Services, Hippo Books, Westfield Road, Southam, Leamington Spa, Warwickshire CV33 OJH*, not forgetting to enclose a cheque or postal order for the price of the book(s) plus 30p per book for postage and packing.